P9-CKY-074

LAUGHTER RING

BOOK TWO OF THE SONG OF THE SEA

LAUGHTER·RING

illustrated by Michael Casad

by
Stephen E.
Cosgrove

Graphic Arts Center Publishing Company

Portland, Oregon

International Standard Book Number 1-55868-032-2
Library of Congress Number 90-82430
Text © MCMXC by Stephen E. Cosgrove
Illustrations © MCMXC by Michael Casad
All rights reserved.
No part of this book can be reproduced by any means
without written permission of the publisher.
Published by Graphic Arts Center Publishing Company
P.O. Box 10306 • Portland, Oregon 97210 • 503/226-2402
Editor-in-Chief • Douglas A. Pfeiffer
Managing Editor • Jean Andrews
Designer • Becky Gyes
Typographer • Harrison Typesetting, Inc.
Printer • Ringier America
Printed in the United States of America

Dedicated to Ani Moss and her tireless efforts to save the lives of our delightful cousins in the sea—the dolphin. You, Ani and the Dolphin Connection, truly are the embodiment of Laughter Ring.

Stephen

To become part and parcel of
The Song of the Sea
please contact . . .

The Dolphin Connection
c/o A and M Records
1416 North La Brea
Hollywood, CA 90028

CONTENTS

GLOSSARY OF TERMS

CLACKER-CLAWS — *Lobsters and crabs of all sorts.*

THE DEEP — *All the waters below the surface of the sea.*

DOLPHINS — *The delight and laughter in the sea. Brethren to the whale.*

THE DRYSIDE — *The land and winds that blow above and beyond the sea.*

FEATHERED FURIES — *An assortment of aquatic birds—seagulls and pelicans—who scavenge for their food.*

FLIPPER-FINS — *Seals and pups. Brethren to dolphin and whale.*

GOLDEN LIGHT — *The light of day.*

POD — *A group or gathering of whales who live their lives in community.*

SANDWALKERS — *Man.*

SHELL-SHARKS — *All forms of boats and ships that carry sandwalkers across the sea.*

SILVERSIDE — *Dark or moonlit nights.*

THE SONG — *The history of the world as sung by the whales.*

TIDES — *Two tides equal one day.*

WATERS OF LIFE — *All the salt waters that make up the seas and oceans of the world.*

WHALE — *A fictitious variety of whales—a bit of Orca, a smattering of Beluga, and the amazing songs as sung by the Humpback.*

WINSOME BRIGHT — *Birthing and raising place of dolphins.*

THE CHARACTERS

GIGGLES
A baby dolphin born in the dryside to Laughter Ring and Little Brother.

HARMONY
Born a white whale—an oddity in the sea.

LAUGHTER RING
Born in a burst of bubbles and filled with laughter, she is the dolphin that tells the tale.

LITTLE BROTHER
A trickster, a jokester who lives with all but laughs at none—the mate of Laughter Ring.

MOMMA LOVE
A plump Beluga filled with love and compassion. Midwife to expectant dolphins and nanny to all the young, she lives alone in Winsome Bright.

NARWHAL OF THE HORN
Mystical whales who are now thought to be extinct.

SHARING
A sandwalker.

"Sing, my children, the song as sung before.
For the singing of the Song of the Sea shall echo beyond
the boundaries of our brief lives and teach the lessons
of the past to those yet to be born in the sea."
sung as part of the song by
Harmony
in the tide 9725

REVUE

The others may sing, and we may listen, but best of all and always, we laugh. And it is we, the two of us, for always—forever and a day. But I am before the story, and the Song of the Sea must be sung clearly to all those who will listen and understand.

This song cannot be sung as some of the other songs have been sung. Those other songs are long in melody and rich in voice. I can barely carry a tune, and my voice squeaks and twitters. The others were whale and were great in philosophy and purpose. I am dolphin, and we have little philosophy. Our purpose as dolphin was and is to laugh, to giggle—to bring mirth and merriment to the cloudiest of days.

I was born long, long ago in a happy time, a time of joy in the waters of life. I lay, like all birthed creatures, for some conscious time in the darkness of my mother's womb, listening to her silly stories about the mysteries of life. "You will be different," she whispered, "You will be special. Your laughter will ring the world and cause rainbows to kiss the waters that flow."

"Who, me?"

Then, in a blink of an octopus eye and the pop of a sea foam bubble, I was suddenly one with the world. Oh, and how the sights and the sounds assailed my senses, but I wasn't shocked or frightened. Like all dolphin, I was amused. The world made me laugh, and laugh I did. I laughed and laughed, rolled and giggled in delight at all I saw

and felt. My mother, the great jokestress (and as tradition dictated) named me on the spot— Laughter Ring.

The mother and daughter intimacy was lost in the riot of colors that danced upon the waters of life. In the silliness of all that is, I immediately joined with others my own age. How the seas rolled with our laughter as we danced on the waves and leaped over the wind. We chased our tails which made us laugh all the merrier, for there were many of the young in those days, and even the older dolphin lived for our laughter.

Time, like the tides, rolled on. We traveled all about the great circle of our sea, from crystal ice to balmy blue, from where the golden light rose in the dawn over the dryside of burning rain to the dryside where it finally fell smoldering into the steamy fields of dryside kelp that waved so oddly there.

Fate always calls to those that listen, and she sang to me in rapture. It wasn't long after my bursting, my joining with the laughter of life, that I met my mate forever more. I was sneaking upon the tuna tails and tickling their bellies from beneath, causing them to scatter in fear, when

"Just me," he sang in his sing-song fashion.

"And just who under the seas is 'just me'?" I asked in mock seriousness.

"My name is Little Brother," he exclaimed in all seriousness.

Whether by reason of his serious tone or perhaps the silliness of his name (I know not which) regardless, I again began to laugh. "Why are you called Little Brother?"

Instantly he turned somber and said, "I must warn you that I am very good at riddles. Why would I not be called Little Brother? Can the answer be a question: Did not my mother and father already birth an older child?"

"And I suppose," I laughed, "that his name is Older Brother. Heaven forbid your parents should birth another son for he should be called Littlest Brother. Then there would be room for no other brothers and your mother would have had to begin on the daughters."

I think at this point the joke had turned a bit sour and my companion of tickle had become indignant at the laughter pointed at his name. "For your information," he retorted tartly, "my other brother is not called Older Brother, but rather something else."

"Like what?" I asked. "Olderest Brother?"

I truly expected a regal name like Prince of the Sea or Radiant Splendor, but he retorted with "Bubble Butt."

Like the pest I was then, I persisted and swam after the bait, "Bubble Butt? Your older brother is called Bubble Butt?" Indignantly, he turned tail to me and I surely felt I had hurt him to the quick. "I am sorry," I sang. "I meant no harm." I swam to him but stayed behind in consolation.

"Yes," he sighed, "you meant no harm but harm you caused."

I found myself the victim of another's teasing. Somewhere, somehow, someone had slipped beneath me and tickled me in the most ticklish of spots between fluke and fin. I giggled and rolled trying to escape as laughter in bubbles fair burst in rainbows in the surface air. Try though I might, I could not escape this demon of the timely tickle.

"Stop!" I cried as unnoticed tears squeezed into the already salty water. "I can laugh no more, or surely I will die."

His voice called to me with the final tickle on my tail. "Be not I the one to cause your death, Laughter Ring that sings so sweet." And there he was—sleek and silver with streaks of black racing back from head to tail.

"Who are you?" I cried, stifling the laughter that yearned to giggle more. "Who tickles those who were made for tickling?"

How the seas rolled with our laughter
as we danced on the waves
and leaped over the wind.

I was hooked, saddened by the laughter turned sour, by the hurt to another. "I truly meant no harm. It was just that the name Bubble Butt seems a bit odd."

He still had his back to me and, I felt deep remorse from my dark humor. "His name really *is* Bubble Butt. He got his name because he was born butt first in a bubble and his butt does look like a bubble." It was then that Little Brother turned toward me, and I could see the mischief in his eyes. He was not hurt at all; he was teasing, a jab in the ribs of some unsuspecting squiggly finned creature.

I was angry and a bit dizzy as one who has been turned round and round. "Why, you . . . ."

"Besides," he laughed, "I really don't have any brother, but I do have a sister called Older Sister. I was to be Little Sister, but nature always causes the rain to fall on those that seek fair weather."

With a flip of his tail under my chin, he was gone in a flash, and I soon chased after him. He breached from the waters as he raced along slicing smoothly into the dryside, gaining speed and distance. I followed, and our spray traced lazy patterns back to the sea.

We chased and chased until my anger turned again to exhausted blows of misted laughter. We finally stopped in a cove of coraled living rock and there we looked long into one another's eyes. It was a deep soulful look that merged and melted all our reserves and, like the others before, we became one—in our own way we were mated for life—bonded by that which must be. Shyly we turned away and joined the others, but we were to be one, soul mates—forever and a day.

In the sea, the tides change, and with changing comes the growth to adulthood. It was strange as I grew how I never felt the change, but rather observed. Little Brother and I bonded closer and closer until we nearly thought alike, which in a way was a scary thought indeed, Little Brother being silly as he was.

Together we played, laughed, and teased the world unmercifully. The feathered furies were a delightful prey and the subject of a great many jokes and games. At times, we would slip slowly beneath them as they floated in the waters of life. Then gently, like a rising tide, Little Brother would rise until one of them would be standing, quite confused, on his back. Not very intelligent were they. They would stand there, these dryside tunas, while I would rise under another one until the two were standing eye to eye. With wide eyes, they would screech warnings to each other and then lumber up into the wind-swept dryside. My friend and I would roll in the seas, bathed in our own laughter.

One of our favorite ploys was to slip into a great gathering of these feathered furies and skim the surface with our fins jutting from the water like some great sharp-fin, which are known to have devoured a feathered fury or two. This cruel joke was played many, many times, but like all jokes, it finally ran its course and became less amusing.

If the truth be known, one day we were playing our little child's game, knifing through the waters pretending to be other than we were, scaring the very feathers off them, when I noticed Little Brother, who was silkily slicing through the water on my strong-fin side. "How smooth he glides," I thought. "Almost like a real sharp-fin."

I swam for a time in this manner with Little Brother at my side, when I dove to change sides and make a new run at the feathered furies. To my amazement, Little Brother had shifted sides, too, and we were still swimming side by side. I blinked and realized that there was no way possible that he could have gotten from one side to the other. Oh sweet water, a real sharp-fin was swimming at my side.

I rose into the water and quickly dove, glancing behind to see if I had eluded whom I had striven so hard to imitate. To my great discomfort, I discovered the sharp-fin had tired of the game and decided to follow me. Not only to follow, but to intercept and perhaps share a small meal—a meal that was composed of me!

I twisted and swam deeper, and yet he followed in that icy way that sharp-fin do. He slid by, as if I weren't there at all, then turned to face me, jaws open wide, glistening teeth in a sickening smile. His eyes rolled and the lids locked in the evil eye of death. This was it! I was soon to be a lump in his stomach. I twisted and lurched to one side as he attacked, knowing too well that my defenses were hardly any defense at all.

My prayers of entrance to the end . . . the beginning were rudely broken as my eye caught a flash of diffused light on yet another sharp-fin.

But this was not another mortal fin; this was none other than Little Brother, and he was throwing himself at my attacker. His body rammed the sharp-fin full in the side, and there was a burst of bubbles as the creature lost a rib or two from the collision. Quickly, Little Brother raced off and attacked, again and again. The sharp-fin soon lost all desire to taste my sweet meat, and beat a hasty retreat into the deep.

I surfaced, my tail quivering in the aftershock of fear that touches all of us at the closeness of a meeting with the beginning of the end. Little Brother soon leaped above and then fell back into the water. His showing off, which normally irritated me, this time did nothing more than ingratiate, as I watched my hero bound about in the waters of life.

Finally he tired of his game and swam over to my side. "Are you okay, my Laughter Ring?" he softly asked.

Surprised by his gentleness, I responded in kind, "I am all right. Thank you. For what you did was very brave and very sweet."

"Not so brave nor for the reason as you would think," he laughed with his eyes twinkling merrily. "For if the sharp-fin had tasted you, he would have spat you out and come looking for me. It is the talk of the sea that I am the sweetest dolphin around." With that, he splashed me full in the face, and the chase was on.

There were also nonliving creatures that swam in our seas—the shell-sharks that carry the sandwalkers onto the waters of life. Throughout our many young journeys around the seas, we came into contact with them over and over again. Some were good, but, for the most part, they brought a sense of wrongness in the sea—something that didn't belong and was best left on the dryside.

We saw the shell-sharks drag behind them great weavings of twisted kelp that trapped all within its confines. To be caught in such weavings meant instant death, for a strong-lunged dolphin needs the sweet air to breathe. At other times, we saw dolphin dragged from the waters of life still full with life, and only moments later, their useless dead bodies were thrown back to us in the taunt and tease of uselessness, proof of our inability to fight the great sandwalkers. Of these weavings, our group as a whole survived. We viewed much and during these times experienced little laughter in the waters of life.

But in life there is always a balance. For every tear shed, there is laughter; and for the dark, there is light. So was it with the shell-sharks and the sandwalkers that rode upon the sea. Little Brother and I had found great sport in chasing the little sun-colored shell-sharks that we called hummers. Unlike the hard-shelled variety, their thin skin was somewhat akin to the whales' hide, but they smelled oddly.

They would wildly race to where Little Brother and I were swimming or chasing tuna tails, and then the humming would stop and so would they. The sandwalkers would sit upon the hummer's back and gaze out for long periods of time to where we played. When we ventured close, they dangled their puny fins in the water as if inviting us to savor the texture and the flavor of their meat. I personally have never tasted them, but there are many tales of sharp-fins who have had one or two sandwalkers for a meal. Thankfully, they were not something that I savored.

However, they were fun to play with, and their antics delighted Little Brother and me almost to the point of tears in our laughter. Little Brother, in particular, recounted to them long, bizarre stories. They would stare intently at him with those eyes that appeared so very intelligent, simulating understanding. Fun to play with, yes; intelligent, no!

But Little Brother would chatter away telling them tales of

*The sandwalkers . . . leaned over
the edge of the shell to reach down
and pet this great white whale.*

flipper fin and tuna tails. They, in turn, would nod their puny heads, moaning their moronic moans, which would send my mate and me into paroxysms of laughter. Little Brother would even at times swipe his head from side to side, splashing them in his irritating way. Their little puny fins would wave furiously, and their moans would turn to squeals, and then they would rush back for more. Not bright, these sandwalkers, definitely not bright.

The innocuous sandwalkers would, on some occasions, even share their food with us. I tried it only once. It was a bit of white, fluffy kelp with a blob of brown glop spread on it. It was horrible! It stuck to the roof of my mouth and surely never had its beginning as flesh. Little Brother seemed to like some of the stuff they tried to feed us, and he once encouraged me to try something he said tasted something like tuna tails. I politely refused.

"Poor little things, the sandwalkers," I used to think, "they give offerings, so in awe are they of us." How wrong I was, not about their intelligence, for I still feel they have little if any, but of their gentle intent.

The shell-sharks came in a variety of shapes and sizes. There were hummers both big and little, some made of whale-like skin, and others of some kind of odd-smelling smooth rock. There were giant hummers that sometimes screamed as they skimmed over the water, and monstrous moaners greater still that groaned their way across the seas.

But of the shell-sharks, my favorites were the silent ones that creaked about in the seas, rocking as the waves rolled. Held above their great shells were flattened clouds that filled with the wind, or sometimes the clouds seemed to just slap at themselves, beating out their distorted rhythms. Often in our young lives together, Little Brother and I sought out these floating islands, for the

sandwalkers that flopped about in them seemed to be a kind lot.

It was great fun to dance in front of these behemoths of the sea, leaping in the froth and foam as they cut laboriously through the water. On one such adventure, Little Brother and I came upon an odd white whale. Of course, we had met whales before in our travels about, but this whale was to change our lives forever, and we would never be the same.

We had been leading a sandwalker carrier on a twisted, convoluted trail through the sea, when just ahead breached a mighty white whale. He was nearly rammed in the side by the shell-shark. My immediate fear was for the safety of the shell-shark and the puny creatures it carried within. Who could know who would survive a collision of that magnitude?

Once again, Little Brother came to the rescue and chanted merrily, "Out of the way. Out of the way. Sandwalkers come looking for fun and they can't seem to find their way."

The whale turned his mighty head, his eyes opened wide in shock, and then he sank like a rock into the deep. Knowing the shell-shark was safe, at least for a time, we swam quickly back to the whale.

He was wallowing in the trough of a wave and muttering to himself, "Where was the warning— the hum, the song that is not a song—that flows with every shell-shark I have seen?"

Little Brother, never at a loss for words, leaped into the whale's soliloquy and answered the question he had not been asked, "This shell-shark is silent. It follows the wind."

"What are you?" sang the whale in a richly accented voice, "You nearly sing the whale song, but you are not whale. What are you?"

"Hmm," laughed Little Brother, "What are I? Well, I are not sandwalker, I are not whale. If I are not these things, then I must be dolphin." With that, Little Brother swam right up to this monstrous white whale and stopped only when he was nearly eye to eye with him. "My name is Little Brother, and that is my mate, Laughter Ring. Our purpose, as dolphin, is to lead the way before yonder shell-shark."

"But why?" sang the whale.

"Why? You of all creatures need to ask why?" Quickly, before the white whale could answer, Little Brother continued his tease. "The sand-walkers that ride the shell-shark make us laugh, and we dolphin live to laugh. Besides, if we didn't lead the way, yonder shell-shark would run over dumb whales like you."

It was my feeling that maybe, just maybe, my mate had gone too far. This whale was ten times our size, and just one little swipe of his mighty tail would send both of us reeling into the seas with aches of the head that could last a lifetime. Many times, we had heard tales that some angry or very hungry whales of this sort had been known to munch upon sharp-tongued dolphin. I rushed between the two of them as they bristled angrily in the water.

"He means no harm," I laughed merrily to break the tension. "He means only to make you smile and laugh at all the fun that spreads beneath the sun."

The whale paused and considered all that had been said. His eyes relaxed and his tone turned from tense to curious. "You say," said he, "that the sandwalkers make you laugh. How can that be? I have seen sandwalkers in their shell-sharks before, and in their wake I have only found death and destruction."

"Oh, 'tis true," continued Little Brother as if there were no threat at all and as if this huge whale were nothing more than some young dolphin to be taught a lesson of life. "Most of the sand-walkers are evil to the very core, but some are fun, and many, in their simple way, bring joy to me on a sunny day. Look, even as we sing, they turn the lumbering shell to follow us."

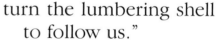

The whale turned his mighty body in the water. Noticing Little Brother was right in his observation, he took a breath to prepare for diving deep. "Never fear, my friend," said I. "They will not hurt you. They are but curious and love to touch all that they see."

The whale looked completely terrified. "Do you mean you

would actually allow the sandwalkers to touch you?" he asked nervously.

"Yup," teased Little Brother, "It doesn't hurt, and besides, it tickles."

The whale lay shaking in the water, scared nearly out of his wits, as the shell-shark drew near. Both Little Brother and I, in an attempt to set the whale at ease, began our usual entertainment of these simple creatures that sailed *upon* the sea rather than within it. We danced on our tails and leaped high into the air, cavorting and throwing laughter at all who would listen.

But the odd white whale never joined us. He just floated anxiously three or four waves away ready to bolt at any moment.

Swimming over to where he lay shaking with fear, I laughed, "The sandwalkers care not about watching us dolphin in our play this day. They are more entertained by you, great white whale. Go to them. Feel their strange dry skin upon your flesh. It will make you laugh, or at the very least, it will enlighten you. Go. These sandwalkers have no evil intent."

The odd white whale looked at me for a long moment, as if for reassurance, and then, because he was challenged with bravery rather than with stupidity, he made his way slowly over to the shell-shark that was standing still in the water, its white clouds that reached up into the dryside flapping in the breeze.

The sandwalkers, following the custom they had established with us, the dolphin, leaned over the edge of the shell to reach down and pet this great white whale. I once again noted their absolute ignorance, for this huge whale could have inhaled one of them with plenty of room left over for a burp.

After a time, the whale relaxed and seemed to be enjoying the stroking and petting. He finally sang to us in his deep, rich tones, "Maybe they, too, have a song but it appears to be an odd song

without depth or soul. Possibly, if I took them into the deep, they would be able to sing their song with more strength."

This innocent statement sent Little Brother and me into gales of laughter. We patiently explained that the sandwalkers knew not how to hold their breath and if they were taken to the deep they would surely drown.

🐚

The whale finally broke away from the shell-shark and called to us. "I must leave, for this is quite perplexing to me. I have been told the sandwalkers bring only death to the sea. Now I see they are not so bad. I must go back to my pod and add this information to our Song."

"Ah," I laughed, "so that is what you are about: a seeker of information." I quickly explained that all the sandwalkers were not as gentle as these and that some, yea even many, bring much death and evil to the sea.

The whale batted his great eyes and looked wonderingly at me and my mate. "Then," he sang, "I must seek out these other sandwalkers that bring evil to the sea. I have many answers that have need of questions to be asked."

Little Brother and I looked at each other and, without even talking it over, chorused together, "We shall guide you if you will have us. For we have traveled far in our journeys and have seen what you seek."

With a flash of our tails, Little Brother and I were off towards the coldest of waters in the farthest reaches of our domain. For if this great white whale sought to see all the evil of the sandwalkers, then we would show him the greatest of their evils. The journey would be far and it would take many tides to accomplish.

We looked back, and it wasn't long before this great white whale joined us on our swim to the cold waters.

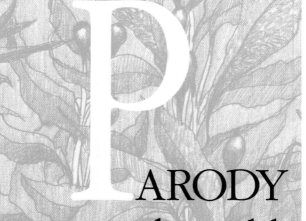

PARODY

We traveled up the seas to the cold waters with our new-found friend, Harmony. Though reluctant to laugh at first, he was truly more in tune with the world than either Little Brother or I. Little Brother loved a challenge, and Harmony was his greatest yet.

My laughter would ring about the sea when Little Brother came floating by with a crown of seaweed or mush-fish on his head. But Harmony would only chuckle a little, at best, and continue on his way. Little Brother told the tale of his imaginary brother and his sister, and although I had heard the story at least a hundred times before, I laughed, but Harmony just smiled. It was only when Little Brother, by accident, got a clacker-claw stuck to his nose that Harmony finally broke down and laughed so hard that he nearly cried.

From that time on, Harmony easily laughed and sang with us as we continued our journey together. He was at the same time both patient and impatient as we swam along. Impatient that we needed an occasional rest, and patient in the understanding that without that rest we all would have to travel slower.

Finally, Harmony asked, "When and where will we see this evil side of the sandwalker, whale, or dolphin. Other than the puny fish we feed upon, the sea is barren of life."

Little Brother sipped a tiny sip of the sea and shuddered in revulsion, "There is a taste in the water of the sandwalker and the evil he brings to the sea. Come next tide, two at the most, you will see that which you won't want to see."

We swam slower now, and the sea was filled with massive chunks of floating crystal water. Early the following tide, we came upon a great group of our distant cousins, the flipper-fins. We happily called to them and were delighted to notice that our big friend, Harmony, too, seemed to recognize the flipper-fin as an extension of the intelligence in the sea. He became excited and before we could tell him the tales of our cousins, he swam quickly away from us to play with them.

It was with horror that we watched Harmony surge into this herd of simple-minded relatives—not to play, but to feast. The herd scattered, dashing up onto the shore, as this great white whale chased a fat cousin into the deep and quickly devoured him in two or three bites at best. We waited—no laughter, no smile—until he swam back to rejoin us.

"What is the matter?" Harmony sang innocently enough, "Is there some evil in the water, some sandwalker drawing near?"

I couldn't even talk so revolted was I, but Little Brother spoke angrily, "You speak of seeking the sandwalker and wish to see their evil ways. Yet you prey on and eat the flesh of our near-to-cousins, the flipper-fins."

Harmony looked at us, his eyes going blank. "That's impossible," he said. "I've never heard them sing."

"You and your songs," I snapped. "Not all are related by a musical song alone. Listen as they speak in the water. Listen to their words so true as they dash in fear of the brutal you!"

The whale paused and listened carefully to the fearful cries of the flipper-fin as they made their escape to the dryside. "I hear not but the bark," he retorted.

"That," said Little Brother, "is the song of the flipper-fin. Whether you know it or not, they are of our family and yours."

The flipper-fin kept singing their song of fear. They sang of that great

white hunter who had killed their leader. They sang a warning in the sea for all to leap to the frozen islands in order to escape the monstrous fiend. It took Harmony a bit of time to realize that he was the great white hunter . . . he was the fiend.

This distant cousin of ours, though over-sized and munch-mouthed, stared at us in total shock-horror as the truth seeped into his dryside brain. His eyes widened, and his skin seemed to pale. He backed away and disappeared for a time into the gloom of the deep. "He makes me a bit nervous," said I. "He talks of lofty ideals and sweet-sung songs and then turns and eats his relatives. I don't know whether I trust him or not."

"I don't know about you," said Little Brother chuckling, "but if I hear his stomach grumbling one more time in hunger, you'll find me flying away with the feathered furies."

Later the great white hunter returned looking for all the world shamefaced, but still I could not trust him. After a time, I quietly whispered to him, "Keep low in the water and watch the shore of the dryside. There you will see part of that which you seek."

We looked toward the shore and watched the flipper-fin that cavorted there, safe from the "menace in the sea." Soon there was movement, and we sighted sandwalkers wobbling swiftly along on spindly fins against the water's edge, as if to pen the flipper-fins farther from the sea. They moved with deliberation and purpose. The larger male flipper-fins were allowed to escape into the water, but the females and the babies were left to their own devices, and the sand-walkers were quite determined that they should have no chance to escape.

The sandwalkers swung their dryside sticks and beat the babies to death. The cries of the young who were dying mixed with the painful agony of the parents who had to watch their children die.

Harmony, after a long time of watching this horror, turned and said, "The sandwalker gathers meat, as does the pod. They are no better or worse than the whale."

"Look again, dear friend," cried Little Brother, as tears traced their way down his silver skin. "The sandwalkers are much worse than you who only seek a meal."

We gazed again at the shore and watched as the sandwalkers ripped the furry skins off the dead children and tossed their carcasses away. Over and over, this was repeated until hundreds of babies were dead and their bodies discarded. Then, as quickly as they had arrived, the sand-walkers left the blood-red beach to the crying mothers and the very few young ones who had survived the massacre.

Unable to help and unable to watch or listen anymore, we moved out to sea to cleanse the filth from our eyes and ears. "I should have snapped the arm from the sandwalker on the shell-shark that touched me before it could do this harm," Harmony rumbled angrily, not even able to sing his message in song.

"It wasn't them," said I very subdued, "for there are many sandwalkers, some are good but most are bad."

We rolled in the silence of the sea, soothed by its very silence. Little Brother and I watched the great whale as he wrestled with all that he had seen. Finally, he roused himself from his intro-spection and said, "Now it is time for me to return to the pod. For I have seen the good and the evil of the sandwalker and there are many lessons that must be sung into the Song."

As much as we would have been glad to be rid of this floating appetite and as much as we wanted to continue our search for delight in the world, I spoke again, "Not yet, my great whale. There is more that you should see."

"More!" he cried in disbelief. "More of the sand-walkers killing the flipper-fin young, and then defying the basest law of the sea by not consum-ing their kill?"

"No," answered Little Brother, "it is worse than that. Much, much worse."

We silently swam down the seas and left the cold, stained waters of the flipper-fin. We didn't talk, let alone sing for a time, out of fear that we might become the next meal for our glutton friend. We ate sparingly of the bottom fish, bug-eye, and flat-tail, and sped quickly down from the cold following the swift currents.

Within a tide or two as the dark turned to light, turned to dark and back to light, Little Brother and I both tried to bring laughter back to the sea. We frolicked and played, breaching over this behemoth, but little could we do to make him laugh. It may have been his introspection of all he had seen, or it may have been that the water changed as the air warmed.

Whenever Little Brother and I swam in this part of the sea, we felt and tasted the wrongness, the bitterness that seemed to seep from the dryside. Often we would have to swim around, or under, a floating island of rot and filth. Objects, the likes of which Harmony had never seen, floated crazily on the water—and because they smelled strongly of evil, a closer inspection was not advised.

Little Brother explained that all these objects and all this filth had come from the sandwalkers that lived on the dryside nearby. The water had become so fouled that Harmony's bright-white skin began to turn an oily black. I jokingly said that Harmony had begun to look like a real whale, but I don't think he was much amused by the transformation. Time and tide again, he would dive to the deep in an effort to rid himself of his stains, only to breach in yet another slick of the brackish, putrid water, and he would be blackened once again.

We swam very close to the dryside and noticed a strange sense and smell of death all around us. Even the fishes had been quite changed and malformed by some devious magic trick that had been performed by the sandwalkers. We pushed on, and in the distance, we finally could hear the plaintive cries of other dolphin. Tired though we were, we swam faster and soon closed in on their pleas for help.

What we found, though so hideous as to be beyond the possibility of belief, were dolphin that were wrapped in kelp-like streamers holding them fast. Some were dead, others were dying. The sea was filled with their screams of torture as the dolphin tried desperately to rip free from their death-bound prison.

Harmony was caught in this death cry and, without thinking of the possible consequences to himself, he tore at these nets of death with his teeth. We feared that he was once again hungry and only sought a quick and easy meal, but we were surprised. He was only trying to free the others. He thrashed about, his great bulk wreaking great havoc with the sandwalkers' woven kelp but, even with all of this tremendous effort, only one was freed. Harmony tried and tried again, seemingly unable to bear the screams of dolphin pain and anguish.

He was finally pushed firmly away by Little Brother and myself. "Try not, our friend," we cried, "for these dolphin have been trapped too long. If they lived, they would be stranger still,

for they have been long without the sweet air to fill their lungs."

We backed away, watching in horror as tens, maybe hundreds, of dolphin died in that cove. Above, we could see the sandwalkers still milling about inside their shells but doing nothing. Soon they began to pull their kelp-like material to the surface, and the dolphin found there that were still clinging to life were beaten until the waters of life ran red with death. Once killed, they were thrown with the fishes up into the shells, an ignominious death.

❦

When all was done and silence returned to the sea, a somber Harmony asked, "Why? The fishes are food for all to share as was commanded by ALL THAT IS RIGHT IN THE WORLD but the dolphin have song. Why do they die?"

"We don't know," Little Brother said, answering in kind.

Little Brother continued, "We think the sandwalkers believe all the fishes to be theirs. We think they don't wish to share, and kill anything that gets in the way. But we really don't know why. We, the dolphin, love all things created, even the sandwalkers, only to be rewarded at times like this with death."

"I have seen enough!" the great white said in anguish. "Now surely you will let me return to my pod to add all these horrors to the Song—to tell of the right and to tell of the wrong."

"No!" I cried. "There is one more that you should see. You must know everything if you seek the truth."

Knowing Harmony's pain at seeing all this for the first time, Little Brother consoled, "It isn't far and it truly is on the way back to your pod." Harmony, so numbed by all that he had seen, meekly followed as we led him back to sea and the sweetness of open water. We swam slowly,

What we found . . . were dolphin that were wrapped in kelp-like streamers holding them fast. Some were dead, others were dying.

commotion. "I must go closer. I can barely see," he protested.

"You don't understand," I quietly consoled, as I leaned into his bulk to restrain him from going closer. "You are in mortal danger here. For the sandwalkers kill not flipper-fin or dolphin. Here they kill the Song itself."

He shook his great head, still without complete understanding. Little Brother came close to his side and whispered, "Here they kill your song. Here they murder whales. All within this pod that swim and sing will die."

Against our warning, Harmony blindly surged forward, brushing us both out of the way like we were some bit of flotsam. We followed to help if we were needed, and it wasn't long before the water turned brown with the blood-sludge of the dead. Around us, strange screaming shell-sharks chased whale after whale and stabbed them deep with pointed sticks. The keening prevailed in the water, but it was not the screaming shells. It was the wordless hum of death from the whales.

We chased after Harmony, and our worst fears were soon realized when a small yellow shell-shark raced madly in his direction with a single sandwalker standing inside. But this little yellow shell was not attacking; it was turning the bigger shells aside. Each one that was turned away meant a whale was saved and would be able to dive to the deep.

We watched helplessly as one of the killing shells suddenly veered away from its course to bear down on Harmony. He stood in the water confused by all that he saw. We shouted, but Harmony was too wrapped up in all the horror around him.

in silence. The great whale sank many times to the deep and soon was cleansed of the filth that had tainted his body. But his memory would never be the same, and the worst was yet to come. As we swam true to the rising golden light, the water seemed to reverberate with keening, a soft high-pitched sound. We swam hard, and the volume of the noise increased until we were bathed in its unearthly sound.

We knew that sound. We understood from all that we had seen before that the carnage to be seen would be beyond that which we could bear. We gently warned our friend, "Go no closer. You must see what you can see from where we are now."

On the horizon, many shell-sharks filled with hundreds of sandwalkers—so large were they—buzzed angrily in the waters of life. Harmony leaped high into the dryside, peering with great intent to discern what could be causing such a

Without thought to our own safety, we began to swim to Harmony with mighty flips of our tails. But even as fast as we were, we could see that the shell-shark would beat us to the mark, and surely he would be killed.

But to both our surprise and our delight, the little, brightly colored shell screamed in front of the killing shell and forced it to veer away from its target. Harmony, at last alert to his danger, quickly dove into the deep and was saved from a cruel and untimely death.

The white whale, numbed and dumbed by all that he had seen, had to be forcibly guided into the cleaner seas. His eyes were glazed with the pain and misery. Harmony quietly sank from our sight, and we politely held our distance, knowing that he needed to be alone to cleanse himself. From the deep, we could hear the keening of his song, and it welled all about us, filling us with its glory.

There is nothing more rapturous than the Song of the Sea when sung in passion. We did not talk, we did not laugh, and it was only by conscious effort that we could even remember to breathe, so beautifully plaintive was the Song as sung by our friend, Harmony.

Finally, the seas were silent again. Soon after, the great white breached from the sea with a roar. There he floated for a bit and, when the silence echoed on the trailing waves, he sang. "I don't know whether to love you for showing me all of this or to hate you forever. My song is filled with confusion."

"Go now to your pod," we said in gentle voice. "Though you be confused, remember that there is good and bad in all things in the sea. You must learn to value each for its balance. Someday we will meet again and share a memory, and we will learn to laugh again."

Filled with sorrow because we understood his great pain, we slowly swam farther down the world to a gentler place. Here we, too, would be able to cleanse ourselves of all the great wrongs we had seen these past many tides.

Although the great white needed to learn these lessons that we taught, it is hard for a dolphin to be without its natural purpose—laughter in the sea. We hadn't laughed freely in gleeful abandonment for such a long time and had need for the clear blue waters of the downside—the corals of Winsome Bright.

As Little Brother and I left our friend, the great white whale, we felt dirty from all the cruelty and horror that we had seen. Try though we might, it did not seem possible to quickly cleanse ourselves of our terrible adventure. The seas were soiled, perhaps forever, and all our senses were clouded and grey.

We swam hard and fast down from the up of the earth towards the warmer waters of Winsome Bright. With every movement, we swam faster and faster, as if speed alone could eradicate the memories etched so deeply.

With muscles working in concert, I darted from side to side and quick-breached to gain even more speed. The grip and ripple of the water as it smoothly crossed over my body made me feel eel-slick and sinewy.

My heart boldly pounded, reminding of mortality, and I pushed even harder, twisting my body in torturous, powerful undulations. I felt fast; and the faster I felt, the faster I swam.

I had always been quicker than Little Brother and loved to challenge him to race after race, knowing the sure outcome of every challenge. He gamely tried to beat me, but rarely did. Even now, as we raced away from both good memory and bad, he was hard pressed to keep up as I slip-breached through the waters, chasing tuna tails and bits of froth.

that I was different from Little Brother and he was different from me. It made me mad at him and at me. This feeling made me swim faster still, and in time I had distanced myself from my mate. My mate? It both angered and confused me. Was he my mate? Always, we had been the best of friends and, as such, we had called each other "mate," but what did it really mean? Were we mates as friends, or friends as mates? Why was I faster than he? Yet why did I feel as though I should be slower and allow him to protect me? Was I to be dominated? Was this what was meant by being female and a mate? Mates: they who subordinate their own feelings to those of the other, their best friend. My mind could only spin round like a waterspout.

I was tired from all the adventures with our new friend, Harmony, yet I was still excited about our travels throughout the seas. We had not been back to the corals of Winsome Bright since birth. The memory of the beginning of delight burned hotly in both our souls and urged us on faster and faster.

But there was change on the tide. Little Brother and I could feel it but really didn't know what it was. The sun still set in purples turned to black, and morning still peeked from wave to wave in a silver wash of golden hush. The fish were sweet to eat, Little Brother was still a fool, but yet there was something odd, not about the water but rather about us.

It was as if I could feel my body grow. I felt longer and sleeker. I felt both vain and embarrassed at the same time. For the first time, I felt

Little Brother finally caught up with me as we arrived at a place where the waters were warm and blue. His breath came in ragged gasps of vented air mixed with laughter. "Why," he questioned, "are you swimming so fast? Are you afraid of some ghost fish, or do you race your tail? A race that can never be won?"

I turned and nipped at his side in anger. "If you can't keep up," said I, "then follow my wake and catch up at a leisure pace like the turtles that wallow in the sea."

He backed away in shock, his eyes turning icy.

"If you weren't such a cloddish clown," I continued angrily but really not knowing why, "and

I found my mind switching
from thoughts of loathing to loving
like the swishing of a sharp-fin's tail.

had learned to swim as a child, you wouldn't have so much trouble keeping up!" I railed.

We swam on, but even so paused at times and slapped verbal insults at one another, there in those waters. Then we would swim sulkingly along again, only to stop and rest—and spit more insults as we swam from the colder, murky seas to the warmer waters. Finally, with eyes squeezed tight in anger, we swam on no longer speaking.

Something was different, and though we never spoke of it, both Little Brother and I felt it. Was this what it meant to get older? Was this the fulfillment of the prophecy, "When you get older, you'll know," made by all parents in answer to insistent questions from their young?

"Now what?" I wondered. "Is up really up or down really down? Is everything changed forever because of some chance meeting we had with a seeking whale? Or is this another mystery, to be solved with, "When you get older, you'll know"?

No answers, but many questions clouded my horizon. I soon found myself loathing my friend that I had known and shared all with since birth, since tides too numerous to count.

Finally, at the end of our stormy trip, we arrived under bright, blue skies at our destination—the corals of Winsome Bright. Our anger—no, truly it was my anger alone that brought on his anger—seemed diffused and softened in this place of magical delight.

We began to zip about in the waters, racing only a breath away from the sharp coral walls to chase bright butterfly fishes that dashed away in fright. This exuberance at reaching our destination put distance on the memories of the horrors and difficulties of the journey, but I still felt charged like the clouds of a loud-noised storm.

I filled myself with the joy of the lagoons and bays, pretending Little Brother was but a pest best forgotten. I swam about this coral sea, amazed as always how fishes changed with the waters, from the deep silvers, blues and purples of colder fish, to pinks, blues, and yellows of the apparently slower, but happier, fishes that were swimming in the warmer waters.

There was a constant celebration of all of life here in these warmer waters, a feeling of a festive tide-to-tide party that had continued since the very beginning of time. This was the feeling, the emotion, that was sensed by all those who entered, all who had ever entered, those magical, coralled pools of Winsome Bright.

Oh, and the memories of a youth long past flooded one's senses with bubbles of joy and ecstasy, as we swam in the warm waters of this enchanted place.

Ridges of coral were rounded about the atolls and tiny islands of the bright side, the dryside. Fishes darted about, playing the silly games that ring true with the survival of all in no matter the water, but here it was funny, here it was a delight.

We swam with the fishes, and chased them in sport and chased them for food. We feasted, and then washed ourselves clean of our anger-filled journey to this idyllic place.

But still and all, Little Brother and I were different, we were changed, and it seemed forever. I felt the need to be in his company, but once there I loathed him and sought to swim away. Once away, I wished only to seek him out again.

I would rush back to his side and breach over him as I had done in the earlier tides of our childhood. He would begin to play, and I would begin to play, and then for some insignificant reason I would turn and order him to go away. I was quite confused about my own feelings and could only imagine what Little Brother must be feeling—although how he felt was certainly no concern of mine. My own feelings were first on, then off, like a waterspout.

Finally he could take no more of my cruelty and angrily rebuffed me with, "Leave me be, little girl. Swim alone in these waters, and if you should find me by accident in some sheltered bay, warn me that you are coming and I will swim away!" With that he surged into the surf and with a flip of his tail disappeared in the foam of an arcing wave.

"Ah, good riddance," said I as he left me alone. "What I need is some peace and quiet." But my words were hollow.

I swam without aim, idling my time by eating constantly of the sweet little fishes when I wasn't even hungry—the ultimate sin of the sea. In this black mood of desperate straits, I came suddenly upon the oddest whale I had ever seen. She was plump, and her eyes twinkled as she watched me streak through the waters of Winsome Bright.

Delighted at last to have someone to talk with besides that dull but clownish Little Brother, I sought her out. "My name is Laughter Ring, and we have come here to Winsome Bright after a long journey in order to rinse ourselves clean of all we have seen," I gushed.

She laughed in a low rolling song and then began, "Ah, my little one, I know. I have listened to you and your mate playing throughout the waters of Winsome Bright."

"He is not my mate!" I tensed. "We have unfortunately known each other since birth, and as friends have called each other mate, but it is only by a twist of fate that we have been together on this journey at all." I paused, embarrassed at my outburst. "Who and what are you?" I asked.

She laughed again, and her sides rolled with the merriment she carried within. "I am a Beluga—the whales of laughter. The others that have come here before you have called me Momma Love."

"Well," I continued, "I am delighted to make your acquaintance, Momma Love. I have found you just in the nick of time, for Little Brother has been swimming me crazy. He is such a baby. All he wants to do is play and make childish jokes. It is good that I am away from him. Even now I can hear him as he swims in play."

"And does that make you happy?" gently asked Momma Love.

"Certainly," I said resolutely, "It makes me very happy that the tuna brain has gone away. It makes me very happy indeed that the bubble-butted, jelly-fished, flat-eyed, sandwalker lover has gone from my life forever. Now I will have a chance for some peace."

Momma Love looked at me with her great soft eyes, gently asking, "But then, why do you cry?"

It was only then I realized I was uncontrollably adding to the salt in the sea. "I don't know," I blubbered. "Everything seems to be changing so fast, and I don't understand what is happening."

Then, like the waters that fall in a rush from the dryside, I told Momma Love all that had happened. I rambled and railed about how I felt about this and that blaming all on Little Brother.

"He's a pain," I cried. "I hate him!"

"Hardly that," she said, as her eyes twinkled. "You don't hate him, but you are in love."

"With him?" I asked incredulously. "How could anyone be in love with a silly dolphin who wears kelp-weed on his head like a crown? Me? In love with a shell-brained fool like Little Brother?" I backed quickly away from this Beluga in shock and revulsion.

"Oh it is true, little one. You are in love and you should not fear that which will come, oh so naturally. Listen, child, once I felt just as you do. Sometimes, I fought that change from childhood to adulthood, and then at other times I tried to urge it to come faster. But all things in time, and in time all things. It is well to wait for complete commitment, for true love, but don't be so blind that you cannot see that which should be."

With that, Momma Love laughed and swam away, leaving me swirling in the wake of all that she had said. "In love with Little Brother? Me? Just wait until I tell him. If ever there has been a joke to be told in the sea, it is this." Quickly, even eagerly, I sought out my old friend, Little Brother, in the corals of Winsome Bright.

I found him sulking in a warm-water tide pool nose-to-nose with a clacker claw. It was only with a bit of gentle teasing that I coaxed him into the deeper waters that surrounded this atoll. I laughingly told him all that had happened. He joined in my laughter as I told him of Momma Love and her hilarious observation that he and I were in love.

It felt so good to laugh again with my friend— my lover. My lover? How did that word slip into my thoughts? What was this malaise that had come over me? Had I become daft? Had Momma Love cast a spell over me to allow such language to seep into my vocabulary?

I watched Little Brother frolic in the foam of the oncoming waves and I had to admit there was a sleekness about him, a muscular grace, that belied his silly nature. I shook my head and spit the thought from my mind. That's it! I was losing my sanity. Little Brother, my lover? Oh, never.

I found my mind switching from thoughts of loathing to loving like the swishing of a sharp-fin's tail. As the golden light dropped into the sea mixing all in purpled splendor, Little Brother inadvertently smoothed against my side. Like the touch of a twisty fire eel, a charge burst from my dorsal to the tip of my tail, and I was changed forever. The waters turned a ghostly blue and light flashed on the waves. It wasn't just me, for in Little Brother's eyes I saw a change, a gentling. A fever set over us and cast our blood afire.

The winds of the dryside were filled with the essence of something from beyond the whispering, golden sands. We paused and gazed into one another's eyes and for the first time, but forever and a day, we saw and touched each other's souls. We became mates, wed on that night of the silverside moon. With the commitment of our souls, we dedicated ourselves to each other and to the will of ALL THAT IS RIGHT IN THE WORLD.

Far out to sea, I sensed a rolling gentle laughter, the gentle laughter of Momma Love.

PAGEANT

We lay enraptured there in those still waters, a bit brighter now, for hundreds of tides. Life took on new meaning. We became bonded and, like the others that had come before, nothing would part us save death. We pledged to live and die together.

Nothing would separate us, not even ALL THAT IS RIGHT IN THE WORLD.

Under the watchful eye of delightful Momma Love, we learned of the joys and responsibilities of adulthood. We were filled with a longing to know more of one another—to join both in spirit and life's direction. What Little Brother would do for the rest of his life, so would I. Where I would go, he would follow. These were more than simple pledges cast upon an empty shore. These vows would bind us for all of eternity.

We had no plans save for our daily needs, but one tide as the skies turned from blue to black, there came a cry across the sea, a faint and plaintive song that was sung far away and echoed in the water, turning its sweetness slightly bitter. It was the final song as sung in the DEATH OF THE THOUSAND SANDWALKERS, the death of an entire pod of whales. Unmistakably, somewhere the Song was sung, and somewhere a great many whale were dying a useless death.

The Song was passionately sung by the pod as they all died in protest of the sandwalker. We may not have sought the source, albeit a strong trait of dolphin is curiosity. But there was another Song,

a Song sung in dirge, a wailing. We had no doubt of the Song's origin. This dirge, this Song was sung by our friend, Harmony.

Without question or word spoken, we left the corals of Winsome Bright knowing somehow we would never return. We swam with an urgency that belied the situation.

The call we heard was filled with such agony, such longing, it could only mean the death of our dear friend. Little Brother led and I followed, gliding in the path he etched in the water, saving strength. Then I would lead, and in that way we were able to cover a great distance in but a tide.

The Song we heard had come a short way across the seas. As close as we were, in less than two tides we approached the great dryside that reared from the waters of life. We searched and searched, listening vainly for traces of the Song, but all we heard were the whispers of others who had gathered in awe at this horrible spectacle.

Near the end of the second tide, we found the babies. Small whales, but there were no mothers here. The little whales circled us and called out short sobbing songs, wanting to be touched even by us, their smaller cousins.

We calmed them as best we could and finally saw that the terrible tragedy had taken place close to the shore where they swam. The babies sang about Harmony, the great white, who had pushed them out to sea when they sought to join the others as they forced their way up onto the dry-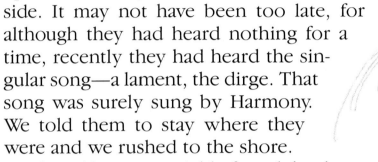side. It may not have been too late, for although they had heard nothing for a time, recently they had heard the singular song—a lament, the dirge. That song was surely sung by Harmony. We told them to stay where they were and we rushed to the shore.

Oh and how we quickly found the devastation. The dryside was strewn with the rotting carcasses of hundreds of whales, but nowhere in the carnage did we find a body cast in alabaster—the white. We rushed from one end of the shore to the other and it was only as we were about to give up that we found his body.

He was pushed up against the shore, and we were sure he was dead. As befitted our friendship, Little Brother and I felt that he, above all, deserved a proper joining with ALL THAT IS RIGHT IN THE WORLD. We began, in concert, to pull and tug on his mighty form. Slowly, this hulk of a body began to move as it scraped back out to sea. Imagine our shock when the body convulsed and seemingly inched back up onto the shore.

We pulled the body out again and once again it shuddered and lumbered closer still. Our shock was compounded when this corpse muttered in a guttural voice, "Ah, no matter. It matters not whether it is a feathered fury or a great sharp-fin

pulling me into the sea as a meal. It matters not; the Song is dead."

I looked at Little Brother and he wide-eyed at me, "He is not dead, at least not of body," I laughed in relief and joy that our friend lived.

"But he is surely out of his mind," Little Brother groaned as he tugged against the behemoth form.

Harmony lurched up onto the shore and we yanked him back. He struggled free and regained all the ground he had lost and then a little more. I was exhausted and mad at this self-pitying mound of flesh. "You blubber brain," I shouted in frustration, "help us, for pity's sake!"

Harmony turned, his eyes half-lidded. "Help us? Help who?" he asked deliriously.

Little Brother mimed his words, "Help us? Help who? Help me? Help you? Come on," he shouted, "help yourself."

He blinked his great eyes, recognition brightening them for a moment, but then they once again slipped into a fogged stupor. "Let me die!" he cried, "for the Song is silent, and the pod is dead!" With that, he flopped higher onto the shore but was still short of his goal.

In a fervor, Little Brother and I yanked him back into the waters of life.

Staring ahead to his self-sought destruction, he wailed like some spoiled child-whale, "By all that is holy, let me die, for all is lost!"

With all of our strength, we yanked him farther into the life-giving waters. "No, not quite all," shouted Little Brother, "for out in the deep wait the children that you saved. Did you simply save them to let them die of confusion?"

We caught our breath, and the seas became quiet save for the distant discordant singing of the children.

"No!" Harmony bellowed. "I am whale and my right is to die as the others before."

"Fine," I taunted, "and the Narwhal are right as they sing. But, what happens when there are no more whale? What happens when all have cast themselves upon the shore? Do you think the sandwalker will feel your protest after you are gone? No! They will push your fat, rotting carcass back to the sea—or better still, leave it where it lies. Then, they will quickly forget and continue with their ruination of the world."

"But," Harmony protested weakly, "I have sung the Song."

"That's carp bile and you know it," snapped Little Brother. "Just who do you sing to as you die? Do you sing to the children, so they can continue this madness? Or do you sing to the sandwalker? There is good reason why the sandwalker does not sing the Song of the Sea. For how can you sing that which you cannot hear?"

He froze in his undulations to reach the dryside. With a sigh breathed deep, he exhaled all that was wrong with his soul and slowly turned his great body back to the sea.

🐚

We all fell into silence as we moved out into the deeper, cleaner waters. No words needed to be spoken, for Harmony was filled with grief, a grief best cleansed with silence. Suddenly, quietly, and without a word, he sank deep into the world.

Little Brother looked worriedly around, "Do you think we should go after him? Does he still mean himself harm?"

"No, I think not," I said, unconvinced myself. "Harmony needs a greater silence than can be provided now. He needs well to talk with himself and learn again to sing the Song of the Sea."

We waited there on the inky surface and nearly gave way to our own fears of his self-destruction, when Harmony breached with such power we were tossed to the sides like foam in a windy sea.

We said not a word as Harmony breathed deep the sweet air that swept the seas. The gleam of life was once again in his eye, and we knew he was resolved to put life in front of him. Together we silently continued our journey from the dryside to find the children who wallowed in the shallow troughs, waiting for someone to rescue them from their plight. After a brief time, we found them not far from shore, confused and so alone.

There were seven in all, four of them female. They sang to us for guidance. They asked for the Song and they asked for food. Fortunately, all but one of them had the first taste of fish and needed not their mother's milk. Little Brother, Harmony, and I swam ourselves ragged, hunting fish and returning to feed the hungry mouths that waited.

Though we tried vainly to feed the littlest one, she was so distraught she would not eat of the fish. Instead, she cried fitfully for the warmth of her mother's milk. Little Brother cavorted about with a tiny tuna tail balanced on his nose trying to achieve with laughter that which nature refused to allow. Still, the child refused to eat. Harmony sang soothing songs laced with hungry messages, but the child would have none of that either.

"What can we do?" the great whale asked. "I can soothe them with song and feed them the fish, but I cannot help this little one."

"It has been done before," I said quietly. "We are both of the family of the sea. I will nurse this young one until she can be taught to eat the fish. It is not much but it will have to do."

"That's ridiculous," snorted Little Brother. "You can't nurse another unless you are great with child." He paused and looked foolishly at me. "Are you . . . are we with child?"

I laughed nervously, not knowing quite how to break the news, "I don't know about you, but I am. If you haven't noticed these last many tides, I have been growing large with child."

Little Brother, my mate, with his eyes wide in amazement swam around and around like a sharp-fin examining a soon-to-be meal.

"But, but," he stuttered and stammered, "I just thought you were getting a little fat. I mean, I thought you were eating a bit more than I . . ."

"Hmm," I muttered as I swam close to the child, "you and I shall talk of this later. Fatter indeed!" Fortunately, the child-whale and I were able to work things out between us, and she quietly suckled. Surprisingly, this sharing—this need and meeting of the need—created a strong bond. I soon felt oddly tied to this child.

Hardly enough to satisfy the young whale the milk did encourage her to try tiny bits of fish. Nourished a bit by both me and the fish, she survived. We whiled the tides, gaining strength and confidence for the young pod.

We moved the small pod around with no goal in no particular direction, waiting for some pronouncement from Harmony as to purpose and cause. The great white whale would disappear for long periods of time and then resurface, dazed by memory freshly swirled.

Finally, one crystal tide as the golden light crept over the edge of the sea, he began to sing. "The Narwhal are wrong. Death is a silent and stupid protest. The Narwhal hide within their frozen crystal walls and give gifts of hate to any whale who happens by, and one by one the whale are

We began, in concert, to pull and tug
on his mighty form.

disappearing. They could do no better if they all gave their twisted horns to the sandwalker so they could kill more of us in the seas.

"They must be stopped and a new Song must be sung. Not a Song sung by just a pod of whale here or there, but all in one massive chorus. And not just the whale but all the brethren, the dolphin and the flipper-fin—all must learn to sing the same Song. And the voice of all shall be strong. For I have a plan, a simple plan indeed that will put an end to the sandwalker as was intended by ALL THAT IS RIGHT IN THE WORLD.

"I shall call a conclave, the greatest meeting of all the brethren of the sea. There shall we sing. There shall be the beginning . . . the end of the sandwalker forever. Go now, my friends. Call your group of dolphin together, and each one of that group shall go to another and another to tell of the conclave. Call to the flipper-fin and the great-backed whale. Call to the blue and the bow head. We shall all meet in five hundred tides in the crystal walls of Narwhal of the Horn."

Little Brother had a tear in his laughter-ringed eye as he spoke, "We shall be three when we meet again: Laughter Ring, our baby, and me. Worry not of us. We shall carry the invitation to sing to all that have the will to hear." With that brief farewell and promises to meet again in the cold icy waters, we swam quickly away.

As the waters rippled around them in wake, I cheerfully chided my mate, "You thought I was fat? In all my years I will never be as fat as your head, you bait fish."

"Well, how was I to know?" said he with a laugh in his voice.

I looked at him in total shock at his naivete. I splashed him in the face and, pretending insult, swam quickly away. It was becoming more of a chore to stay ahead of my slower mate, but I was swimming for two. Little Brother easily caught up and said a quick, mumbled, and squeaky apology.

Then he splashed me full in the face, and the laughter returned to our journey as we sought the others. For the conclave of all who sang in the sea was to be the greatest event ever since the beginning of ALL THAT IS RIGHT IN THE WORLD.

❦

We traveled first down the world and were constrained, as if the child I was carrying was some frightening mystery. With the passing of the tides, Little Brother once again began to act with the same reckless abandon of our idyllic days in the corals of Winsome Bright. He was a bit gentler and not quite as rough when we played the simple games that made us dolphin.

I loved all the laughter and the games Little Brother invented, for if anything, I played even rougher than before. Often I would flap water full in his face with my tail for no other purpose than to hear him squeak in shock and delight at the deception. Fat indeed!

This child bearing was a great lark, but there were some little things that caused me a bit of dismay. The child growing within me took away from my sleekness and also interfered with the smoothness of my swimming. For the most part, I felt I was swimming like a rock.

My dives, however, did become things of great power. I could quickly drop into the deep, leaving my mate far behind. The return was an entirely different matter. Little Brother and I would surge up, and he would leap into the dryside in a great, powerful, rainbow arch. I, on the other fin, would surface only to flop back to where we belonged. Not quite a thing of beauty and grace.

To compensate for the extra weight I was carrying, I began to eat more and more to add body fat, in theory—my theory—to increase my buoyancy. I would eat anything and everything: the firm fish that are sleek of skin and bright of eye, the twisted legged squid, and also the slow and somewhat dull-eyed bottom fish that tasted like mud but were filling just the same.

The odd thing was that everything tasted absolutely delicious—in unusual combinations, and in great quantities. I'm sure Little Brother was dismayed and slightly disgusted with me, but what was I to do? Everything tasted so good.

I came even to love the taste and texture of the long, floppy kelp, which normally no self-respecting dolphin would eat. In shock at my unusual diet, Little Brother would turn the color and hue of a stormy sea and swim away. I found myself eating alone quite often. It all tasted so good, and the extra fat did help me float, though like a water-soaked bit of dryside wood.

Now I not only swam like a rock, I began to look like a boulder. My body dynamics took on the properties of a sandwalker barge. The message carried by Little Brother and me was of extreme importance to all that lived in the sea. My mate would dash ahead, then return constantly to check on my progress. He would usually find me chugging along, with my cheeks both plump and pumping, as I munched upon this and that.

One tide, in the bright of the morning sun that warmed our sides as we swam, he said, "I know that you are great with our child, but we must find some way to hurry on our way or the conclave will be sung, and all we will hear is a vague echo in the sea."

"But I am doing all I can," I argued. "Perhaps you could help?"

"And how would you best propose, my sweet dolphin, that I do that? Should I drag you through the seas with a bit of kelp? Or maybe you wish that I would carry you on my great back?"

"Hmm," I reflected in jest, "your back may be great but I am afraid not great enough for the child and me. Maybe you could give a ride to a tuna tail, something more your own size?"

I must have insulted him with my pregnant humor, for he swam ahead and soon disappeared. I lumbered along, my wake wide and without definition. Soon I was shocked to feel myself lifted slightly in the water, and there I was swimming at great speed.

Below me, I could feel the strong undulations of Little Brother as he tried vainly to accommodate my wishes. I could feel, rather than hear, his laughter bubbling beneath me. Together, we finally crashed through a wave and were left giggling in the surf and foam.

We rolled in the water nosing and slapping each other. Our laughter was frozen in mid-giggle by dolphin voices. In our frolic and play, we had

broken the perfect formation of a regimented group of needle-nose dolphin, the strictest and most organized in the sea. We settled down, feeling a bit foolish.

"I'm sorry," said Little Brother, gathering his composure as best he could. "We are on a journey to tell all that live in the sea of a great gathering of all the thinking creatures of the sea."

The leader of the group turned away from us as Little Brother told the tale as sung by Harmony, the great white. Little Brother told of all that had happened with the Narwhal and the great journey we had undertaken. He told of good and not-so-good sandwalkers and he told of the beaching of the whales and the death of all. Finally, he told of the called-for conclave of all thinking things in the sea. When he finished, the sea ran silent.

Finally, a wrinkled, narrow female spoke, "All this sounds very good from two dolphin who cannot think two serious thoughts in a row. Could this be no more than a fabrication to bring you laughter? How do we know whether you tell us nothing more than fun-filled lies?"

"Yes," the others chorused prudishly and prudently. "How do we know that you do not lie?"

I was ready, as was Little Brother, to bash a few heads to convince this group of the truth of our words, when our intentions were interrupted.

"Because they tell the truth!"

I spun to see our champion, only to be brushed aside by the leader of the group. "These dolphin, silly though they are, do speak the truth. I have heard the Narwhal sing in the colder waters. I have seen the whales crawl up onto the dryside to die in protest. I have seen all the destruction wrought by the sandwalker. I lost my mate to a shell-shark that carries the sandwalker into the sea. I will join this conclave!"

Anger turned to relief as our truth was known. Laugh though we may and silly though Little Brother and I be, the truth of our words shall never be sullied. This odd pod of dolphin, in their strict formation, promised to carry the message as they made their way up the seas to the conclave. It was with relief that we bid them farewell, but not until they admonished us again for our silliness when we should have been serious.

We swam in solemn silence continuing our journey. Finally we both broke into laughter, and the seas rang again with our joy.

❦

We continued on but it was becoming more and more evident that in my advanced state of pregnancy, I was holding us slow in the water. Little Brother began to rush ahead crying out his message to any and all who would hear. Finally, he came rushing excitedly to me.

"Come, my fat bride," he laughed merrily, "I have found you a ride."

Curiously, I followed. He surged ahead, and soon we came upon a great shell-shark plowing through the water. I was shocked to see Little Brother rush to the front of the beast. There he threw himself in its path but, instead of being run over, he was carried along by the great wave it created as it hacked its way through the seas.

So this was his ride for me. With a giggle, I soon caught up with the ponderous shell-shark and placed myself beside Little Brother in this great shell-made wave. I was carried along effortlessly, and with an occasional kick or two, I would stay there, racing along at great speed.

We glided this way, exhilarated by the effortless speed, shouting to all of the coming conclave. The message was received by a small pod of whale here, and groups of dolphin and flipper-fin there, as we moved along. Unfortunately, all good things soon come to an end. When the great shell-shark reached shallow water, precursor to the dryside, it slowed and then nearly stopped. Our free ride ended.

We had broken the perfect formation of a regimented group of needle-nose dolphin. . . . We settled down, feeling a bit foolish.

We began to swim once again on our own, but it was obvious I was slowing us down to near wave-like speed. Finally, I stopped and cried to Little Brother who had rushed ahead.

He swam back to me, and I said, "My mate, my love, this message is too important. Go and tell all who would hear and have them tell others. I will wait near the dryside, and when you are finished come back for me. Together we shall move up the seas to tell others and join the meeting."

Little Brother protested about my safety but I quickly convinced him that I would be safe. It was only after much arguing that he reluctantly agreed, and after much cuddling, he resumed the quest alone but unencumbered. I laughed at his warm memory as I whiled the hours and tides, ever moving closer to shore where the feeding was easy.

On the seventh tide, several yellow bounce-skinned shell-shark-hummers came buzzing into the waters where I fed. I was much accustomed to the sandwalkers and their odd craft and feared them not at all, knowing I could easily escape if they became over-friendly. Besides, Little Brother and I had taught Harmony that some of the puny-finned sandwalkers were but curious to touch us.

The hummers buzzed about, but they were always just over there, and there, and there. It was with much consternation that I realized they seemed to be everywhere. Still I felt safe in the knowledge that I could out swim them if the need should arise, and I continued my shallow feeding.

A brief time passed, and suddenly I knew that something was amiss. The shell-sharks moved slowly upon me, circling in tighter and tighter circles. I swam this way and they swam this way. I swam that way and they swam that way. I couldn't dive beneath them for the water was too shallow. I decided to charge at them, then veer off between. In that way, I would gain the open seas.

I rushed at them, then at the last moment, I dove and was shocked nearly out of my wits to find myself tangled in strange kelp strands I could not break. I struggled, only to become wound in these unnatural nets.

I struggled and tore at the captive kelp, but only succeeded in using all my reserve of sweet air, and my strength ebbed fast. I needed to breathe.

I twisted and turned in the effort to free myself, but to no avail. I prepared to die and to return to the end . . . the beginning.

Little Brother, my mate, my friend, I loved you. . . .

BURLESQUE

My death was short-lived and somewhat premature. The tough kelp that trapped me beneath the surface was stripped away, and puny little fins guided me to the surface. When I was yanked from the water, my lungs worked without my wise guidance or counsel.

Giving an involuntary gasp, they filled with sweet air. All my senses returned in a flash of black to red to white to light. I was quite surrounded—captured, if you would—by seal-skinned sandwalkers who swam in the water with me.

A skin of some sort had been wrapped around me, and I was quite unceremoniously lifted above the sea and dropped into the shell-shark. I had seen the inside of one of these strange creatures before when Little Brother and I had breached above its sides, but nothing prepared me for the actual experience of riding on its back.

I lay perfectly still—partly from fear, partly from curiosity about my surroundings. The back of this creature swarmed with puny-finned sandwalkers who rushed about doing odd things to odd things. Some would bend down beside me and look me in the eye and utter some strange whistles punctuated with guttural burpings (and Little Brother thought my singing unharmonic).

From deep within this hard-shelled creature's bowels, I could hear the buzzing and groaning of its insides straining from its great mass. It began to pitch and yaw in the open sea, and I could tell that it was attempting to swim.

The sandwalkers now regularly leaned down to touch me as was their desire and strange satisfaction. Still others splashed me with water from the sea, as if to say, "It's all right; the seas are still with you." Then they did the oddest thing: they smeared my body from nose to tail with sickeningly sweet melted jellyfish.

Then for no apparent reason, they placed a very cold and long-dead fish in my mouth. Did they really wish that I would eat such filth? I spat the dead thing out. They pushed it back in. I spat. They pushed.

Foodfight!

I looked up and could see an odd spirit burning in the eyes of my captors. This fish dance must be some ceremony of great religious significance. I finally relented and swallowed the fish whole.

In this manner I was fed three dead fish, and somehow this satisfied these odd sandwalkers. They asked me to eat no more.

I didn't see much as the shell-shark swam, but the sounds and smells of the sandwalker assailed my senses. The beast settled into a steady stroke as the smells grew stronger and the sweet scent of the sea was replaced by other unidentified scents.

Suddenly the shell-shark went silent, though we were still in the water.

But all that had happened was soon forgotten as the air was filled with a heavy chopping sound. The wind stirred about me; the strange wispy seaweed on the sandwalkers' heads blew this way and that. I could see nothing forward other than puny fins and the armored skin of the shell-shark. I looked up and to my horror, there above was the largest feathered fury I have ever seen—if indeed it was a feathered fury at all. It looked something like a shell-shark but with a great fin that spun crazily about.

Hovering above me for a time, the metaled fury's whomping sound pulsed the air. Finally it dropped a large coil of kelp to the back of the shell-shark. Then the skin on which I lay was twisted in the kelp, and with a slap on my back, I was lifted into the air with a lurch, a captive of this shelled feathered fury.

Finally, I knew what was to happen. I was to be fed to this great bird of stone. I waited for that moment I would enter the belly of that great beast and truly and finally be joined with the end . . . the beginning. Strangely though, I was not eaten, but, instead, I was carried to great heights, lifted clear up into the clouds.

Higher and higher I was carried, but I refused to look up any- more and cast my eyes down to the sea. Lo, what a world! The dry- side seemed filled with

straight-lined mountained corals that reached for the sky but with no water to surround them. I yearned to see more of these strange miracles, but we left the coral mountains and moved ahead with the sea on one side of the shell-shark and the dryside on the other.

As the huge metaled fury moved slower, I could see odd islands of water trapped in coral pools surrounded by the dryside—the opposite of all I had known. It was to these dryside water islands the great bird dropped, and I was sure that here was where it nested and kept its young.

Ah, ha! That was it! I was to be fed to the young of this flying monstrosity. As if in answer, the beast dropped lower and lower, until I was nearly touching the dryside. But instead of finding my- self pounced upon by hungry, hopping, metaled furies, I was instantly surrounded by sandwalkers

I lay perfectly still—partly from fear, partly from curiosity about my surroundings.

who gently guided me to a soft landing on a raised slab of cool stone.

With fins all around, they pushed me, and I glided on past the smooth coral and rock into the dryside itself. Away from the golden light I had always found darkness, but here in the land of the sandwalker, the golden light seemed trapped in smooth water orbs that glowed like the light of day. On and on I was whisked through the walls of stone that opened with crashes and clanks. At last, I was stopped in a great room filled with acid smells and strange plants that grew in odd directions.

I began to panic and flipped my body mightily against the restraints. A sharp stinging pain distracted me on my right side, and suddenly I could not move at all, save for my eyes. But I could feel, though numbly, the length of my body. Every bit of my surface skin was poked and prodded: my eyes, my vent, my tongue and teeth. Nothing was left unexamined.

And then these creatures, long cast from the sea, became quite excited. They began to whistle and burp faster and faster. They all rushed from my sight, yet I was still able to hear them. In a way that only a mother could understand, I knew they had found my baby, the child growing in my womb, and there was a wonder about them.

Reverently now, a sandwalker with gentle eyes and long seaweed draped from its head came to gaze. We stared at one another for the longest of times, and I reached out with my heart, beseeching it to set me free. But sandwalkers cannot sing, and those who cannot sing cannot hear the Song as it is sung.

There was more poking and prodding, then some new sharp stings. My skin began to tingle as life was given back to me.

After a time, I once again glided through the strange narrow canyons and, once again, into the non-captive light, that golden light of the true day.

I was lifted again and felt the comfort of those waters of life wash me as I was put back in the water. I breathed deep and thought I could almost smell the sweetness of the open sea. But this strange water, oddly enough, seemed *too* clean. Was I actually free? I cast a sounding cry, but the echo returned coldly from all around. I realized I was trapped in a captive water island completely surrounded by stone and coral.

I swam about this pool of sterile water faster and faster, seeking escape, but none was found. I breached and leaped from the water over and over again to further view my strange surroundings. All I could see were other pools and sandwalkers standing around, gaping.

For how long I spun in that pool I know not. The skies turned first to pink, then purple, then black. The blinking lights of night winked at me just as they had done in other places, other times. Suddenly, in a flash of blinding light, I was back in the bright light of day. But no, it was not the sun, but rather, strange crystal orbs that had captured bits of light and now brightly flooded the pool in which I swam.

I moved to the center of this dryside pool, lying there still for the longest of time, and the sandwalkers moved away one by one on their puny fins. Then, as quickly as the light of day had come, it disappeared, and I was plunged into the cool, soothing darkness of the silverside night.

I called out, hoping against hope that a pod close to shore might hear, but I was rewarded only by the echoing of the water on the smooth rock shores. There was no one to hear me in my plight. There would be no dramatic rescue. I was trapped, captured in some nightmare dream, ripped from my home, my life, the sea.

I shouted out in my fear and anger, but there was no Little Brother to soothe me. In desperation at the joke I had played on myself, I laughed, and then I cried.

I slept fitfully through the night, and as morning's true light crept across the stone ponds, I was awake and searching for some opening that might afford my escape. Search though I might, I found nothing other than the bubbly source of the sterile water. I leaned into the stream of bubbles, but I could smell no trace of the open sea, only unnatural scents. Oddly enough, the water burnt my eyes.

When I finished my simple morning exploration, I heard the others. There was faint whispering, barely echoing through the dryside from the other ponds, but they were there. There may have been four or five individual voices of dolphin and even one of whale. They seemed excited in an unfearful way but they lacked the deep feeling, the emotion, the passion of the others that I had known in the open seas. After a while, things settled down, and I could not hear the whisperings anymore.

In a frustration born of boredom, I swam in the widest circles possible, more than anything because I felt

the need for exercise and the chance to relieve the pains of the cramps the baby was causing. I had not swum for long when there came an odd clicking sound, followed by the splash of something thrown in the water. I sourced the object and, by its size, I knew it must be a fish. I surged down to it and was shocked to find another of those long-dead fish so favored by the sandwalker.

"Why do they do that?" I wondered. "Is it some sort of game for the sandwalker to throw dead fish at dolphin?"

I nosed the fish around the pond, trying to revive it, when the odd clicking began again. There was a splash, and another dead fish joined the collection.

"This is getting ridiculous," I spoke out loud. "What am I to do with these?"

But I knew truly what they were for—they were to be eaten. For the sake of the child, for the sake of myself, who was very hungry, I ate the very dead fish. In truth, it wasn't that bad; it was worse. When the second was eaten, the odd clicking came again, and another fish, and another were thrown into the water.

It was obvious where the fish came from; what was not obvious was the meaning of it all. Why were they attempting to feed me? Why did they trap me in the first place? What did they want? What was the game?

After I had eaten my fill and the last two fish were left to rest and sing their silent song on the bottom of the pond, the strange clickings stopped. I was alone with the solitary sound of slapping water on smooth rock shores. The walls of the pond reared half my length up from the lapping water, which made it nearly impossible to see anything on the dryside, and there was much dryside to see.

There was nothing to do, save swim a round or two of the pond which I had already done, so I tail-walked high on the water and looked over the rock edge of the pool. What a surprise! A group of sandwalkers swarmed together just on the other side of the wall, watching me. I don't know who was more shocked—the sandwalkers or me. I quickly backflipped into the water.

But why were they staring at me?

Before I could ponder much, the sandwalkers made their way to the edge of the pool, gawking with their odd, dry-blinking eyes. Seeing them stand there watching, I was overwhelmed with anger. They had taken me from the sea. They had taken me from Little Brother. They had taken me from all that I loved.

I leaped in the center of the pool and circled underwater, pausing for a moment below the spot where the sandwalkers watched. I swam around again and again gaining speed, then breached as high as my plump body would allow. My plan was to slam one of them full face with my tail, but the best I accomplished was to wash them clean.

I back-swam with my head out of the water, angrily berating them for what they had done. "You slime-gutted jellyfish. You eggs that were never hatched," I ranted and railed. From the dryside came the burbles and burps of excited sandwalkers. Maybe they liked the water. Using my front fins, I tossed more and more water at them, hoping to wash just one of them into the tank to possibly have a little chat, but all that happened was that the sandwalkers were forced back from the slick-stone shore.

Every time they returned to the edge, I rewarded them with vertical rain, but soon even I tired of this game and retired to the center of the pool. As the day went on, they, too, tired of just watching. A few of the sandwalkers drifted away, and others dragged things to the edge of the pool. Then the clicking began again.

"But that is enigma," I protested. . . . "You
don't want to be here but yet
you stay of your own free will?"

code in what they were saying, my understanding was awfully slow in coming.

The sandwalker at least kept my captivity interesting with bits of junk that they threw in the water. I examined it all carefully, searching for the answer to what the sandwalker wanted of me.

But what odd junk!

There was a red-skinned orb as round and as smooth as a water-washed stone, and also a flat circle with a hole in the middle that seemed made of a strange floating skin. There was also a larger circle which they suspended over the pool vertical to the water and the sky.

I threw whatever the sandwalkers tossed to me back at them. My hope was that I might hit one of them full in the face, but if this creature had a special ability, it was an adeptness in the way it could use its puny fins, and it managed to catch all of my ill-timed missiles.

Oh, how I wished for just one of the floating, poisoned jellied fish. That would indeed give them something to catch.

The circle that they suspended above the pool will always be a mystery to me. The best I can figure is that it held some religious significance. Once I even jumped through it, but the sandwalkers became so agitated, I avoided that practice in the future.

My other problem was that I was becoming more and more pregnant every tide, and escape, though seemingly impossible, was always foremost in my thoughts. I continued to eat the dead fish that were thrown into the water, for there was

What did it mean? I listened to the tonals echoing in the water. There was a faint, very faint, resemblance to the crudest of speech, but it sounded like no singing creature I had ever heard before. If those repeated clickings were some odd kind of speech or song, they obviously meant very little. Freely translated, they meant "squid giggle." But was this some kind of code? Were the sandwalkers trying to communicate with me? Did they think I was a squiggle-fin?

This strange communication did not continue night and day, for there were long periods when nothing happened at all, but the return of the sandwalkers was always preceded by the clicking words, "squid giggle." During the long nights when I was unable to sleep, I would replay the noises and actually reached the point where I could imitate the sounds. If there was a secret nothing else to eat. The smooth stone pool was devoid of all life.

⬤

It was some tides later that an opening mysteriously appeared at one end of the pool. As I sounded the entry looking for lurking danger, I heard the most delightful sound—the clear, crisp callings from others of my kind.

With strong pulls of my tail I surged into the pool's entry, through a darkened cave I seek-sensed was devoid of obstacles, and into a larger pool where I found the others—or rather they found me. Suddenly, I found myself surrounded by five exuberant dolphin and one fat whale.

"Thank ALL THAT IS RIGHT IN THE WORLD," I gushed. "I am not alone."

"Of course you're not, dearie," said a wrinkled old dolphin. "We are all here together."

"How wonderful!" I babbled in a rush. "Among the six of us—seven counting the whale—we should be able to find a way of escape."

The old dolphin looked at me and laughed merrily, "Why ever would we try to do such a foolish thing?"

"Yes, whatever for?" the rest chorused.

I looked at my fellow prisoners in total shock. "Do you mean to say that you *want* to stay here? You would rather stay here as captives than be free in the open sea?"

The fat whale laughed, and his sides rolled and undulated in a merry fashion. "Oh, no, no, no," he laughed. "That is to say, we don't really like it here, and we don't really want to stay here. We would much rather be in the open sea, but we still remain here of our own free will."

"But that is enigma," I protested as I shook my head searching for some bit of logic. "You don't want to be here but yet you stay of your own free will? For pity's sake, you were all captured like I was, and yet for some strange reason, you wish to

stay? You, my friends, have eaten too much of the dead fish."

"Oh, my poor, sweet dear," the old dolphin said as she tried to console me, "Do you really mean to say that you were caught and didn't want to be caught?"

"Of course," I snapped, trying desperately to make sense of their riddle-like questions that were offered as answers to my questions.

"Listen, my sweet," softly spoke the fat whale, "have you noticed certain odd things as you've been detained here? Certain odd things about the sandwalker?"

"Certainly," I snarled. "I have heard the odd clicking that is almost speech before they throw dead fish at me. I have noticed how the sandwalkers stare and stare. But what has all this to do with you and me?"

The other dolphin settled themselves in the water, and the fat whale began to sing, "We have discovered over recent tides that sandwalkers, though they don't know the Song of the Sea, wish to sing it. They don't have the heart, and yet some of them possess the spirit.

"Many, many tides ago, a mysterious pod of whales, the mystical Narwhal, decided to make contact with the sandwalker. They sought out volunteers to be captured of their own will. Once captured, they were to learn of the heart of this odd and sometimes evil creature that refuses to acknowledge the Song of the Sea.

"For thousands of tides, we, the dolphin, the whale, and even our crude cousins, the flipper-fin, have given ourselves up for capture. While penned and locked in these sterile surroundings, we study the sandwalker. As each new member is added, we sing this detailed song so that all can share the knowledge that we have gained while in voluntary captivity.

"At times one or more of us either escapes or has been set free. The information all of us have gathered is taken up to the Narwhal in the colder waters. The Narwhal assimilate the information into their song and pass that information along with the litany of ALL THAT IS RIGHT IN THE WORLD. They, in turn, sing to any who come near and further the transfer of the truth to all who would hear of it."

I twisted in the water both by a child-cramp and by the shock of what the fat whale had said. I quickly told them of everything that had transpired and of the conclave that had been called of all those who swim in the sea. Finally, with tears in my eyes, I told them of my mate, Little Brother, and of the child I now carried. I told them of my loss of free will as I was stolen from the sea.

"Oh, my sweet dear," the other dolphins cried, "you are with child. This will make it more difficult, but we will see that you are freed."

"You talk of freedom and of escape," I spat as I stifled my tears, "but I have seen these stone pools, and there is no escape."

"True," the old dolphin said, "but in tides past, small whale and dolphin are put in our midst to grow in strength, and then, for some strange reason we have never understood, the sandwalker takes them back to the sea."

"But if that is true," I continued, "then I might be imprisoned for many tides before they decide to set me free! The conclave comes soon, and I have to carry what you have said to Harmony."

The fat whale's eyes narrowed in deep concentration as he added my tiny melody to his version of the Song of the Sea. "If what you say is true, and I have no doubt that it is, then it is important that you are set free. Here, we have found something that will shake the very melody of the Song itself. You see, we have discovered a sandwalker that not only has soul but she can understand and now sings, though crudely, the Song of the Sea."

My mind raced with the possibility, but I knew there was no way it could be true. The crude sandwalkers—known to be the source of all the evil in the sea—simply could not know the Song. My fears and doubts I spoke of quickly.

"It is true, that which the whale has sung," the old dolphin said firmly, "I have been here longer than any of the others and I, too, have heard the sandwalker sing."

"But," I protested, "I have heard the crude clickings in the water. The best I have been able to make out is that they can say 'squid giggle' which makes no sense at all to me. This can hardly be called the singing of the Song."

The fat whale continued, "This sandwalker does not listen to the other sandwalkers, nor for that matter does she truly hear our Song. But rather she feels, with her fins and her whole body when immersed in the water, the Song as sung by the whale and the stories as told by the dolphin. By our standards and the standards of the sandwalker, she cannot hear a single word spoken or sung. Although she is totally deaf, she is filled with the gift of spirit."

I thought about all they had sung, then countered with logic of my own, "If this sandwalker cannot hear, but in some way senses and feels the Song, how can she sing? We all know that those who cannot hear, also have no voice."

"She sings with her fins an odd song. Though this seems strange, we are able to understand her, and she us. We are unable to speak or sing her name as the sandwalker does in the guttural burpings, but we have given her an honor never before bestowed on one who swims on the dryside. We have given her a place in the Song of the Sea. We have given her a name."

And then together the five dolphin and one fat whale sang, "She is Sharing."

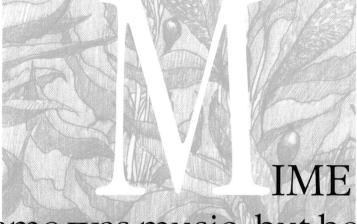

MIME

Sharing. The name was music, but her fabled actions would have great impact on all who sing the Song. If she could do as they said, it was imperative that Harmony have this information before the conclave. If one sandwalker could sing, others might, too.

I needed to escape soon, but first I would have to see and hear with my own heart the Song as sung by this sandwalker . . . Sharing.

Our gathering was rudely interrupted by the sandwalkers' strange clicking in the water. "Squid giggle! Squid giggle!" the clicking called.

"Is that all they know how to say?" I asked, shaking my head.

The fat whale's body shook and rolled like a jellyfish in wandering seas as he laughed, "Just about. I really don't think they know what they sing. But they are pleased that it gets our attention. Come! We are being called. You will like this. For we now dance for the sandwalker, and in their laughter, you will learn a lot."

The group moved to the other end of the great pool and dove. I followed suit, and there below the surface was another opening like the one that had appeared in my tiny pond. The sound of the clicking became louder as I dove through the cave. I surfaced in a small sea, a pool scrubbed clean and colored in the almost-true colors of the corals of Winsome Bright. In the center of the tiny sea was a smooth, stone island. A strange sound emanated in rhythmic pulses that were felt in the water. Objects, like those that were thrown in my small pool, were scattered about.

But I was taken aback not by what I had seen in and around the pool, but rather by what was on the outside. Beyond the pool there rose a great mountain filled with ridges, and on these ridges were sandwalkers—hundreds and hundreds of them—the largest pod I have ever seen. They were slapping their puny fins together like the flipper-fins sometimes were wont to do.

The air was filled with their roarings. The only thing I could compare the feeling to was the blood-fever that the sharp-fins fall victim to as they go to the kill. My most immediate fear was that this was the sandwalkers' feeding time and we were their meal.

The old dolphin moved close to me and called loudly so that I could hear over the roar, "Stay back against the edge of the pool and watch. If you like laughter, even in this captive situation you will find yourself amused."

"Where is Sharing?" I shouted back. "Is she here, too?"

"She is here and watching but truly not a part. When all this is over you shall meet her, fear not."

I did as I was told and began to watch the greatest spectacle that I have ever seen. It started with two of the dolphins leaping through large rings supported over the water. As they leaped high into the air, all of the sandwalkers became highly agitated, slapping their fins and stomping their split-tails. The air filled with whistles and clicking, such as I have never heard before, and will likely never hear again.

As two dolphin swam about and again leaped through the rings, yet another dolphin breached high into the air touching the fin of a sandwalker bal-

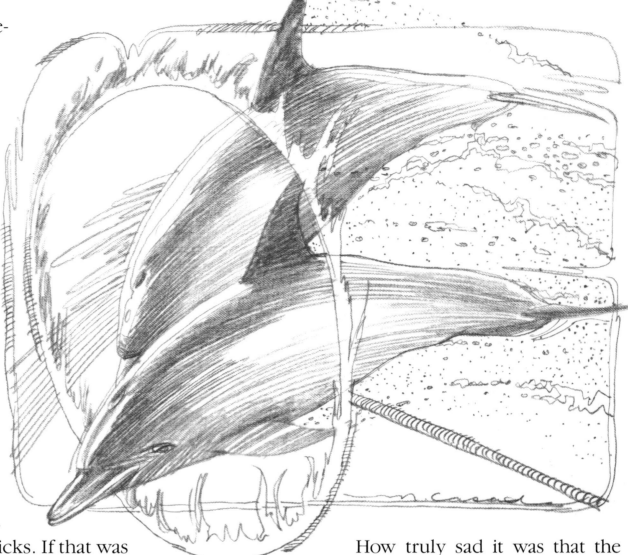

anced on one of the great sticks. If that was not enough, as soon as he returned to the water, three dolphin tail-danced across the pond.

All the dolphin were laughing and calling encouragement to one another as they bested each other's tricks. They even beached themselves on the slick-shored island and lifted their tails in welcome. All of this was greeted by a greater and greater frenzy from the sandwalkers that reclined on the great mountain.

And then I heard, or rather at first felt, the great laughter and joy of these strange creatures of the dryside. Suddenly, it all made sense, for these dolphin were not captives at all. They were bringing to these sad dryside creatures, who would never know the joy of the sea, a gift—a gift of the laughter and freedom they would never be able to experience firsthand.

How truly sad it was that the sandwalker must live its puny life as a voyeur, one who only finds happiness by watching others enjoy. It was no wonder that they, for the most part, had never learned to sing and had been cast from the sea by ALL THAT IS RIGHT IN THE WORLD.

The waters seemed to ripple with excitement. The dolphin raced about, leaping in synchronization and breaching over and over again. Even the fat whale beached himself for a moment and then after a side-long wink to me, dove to the deepest part of the pool to be forgotten for a moment by these sandwalkers. All five of the dolphin tail-danced about the pool and then they, too, dove, and the waters became still. Even the lowly sandwalker quieted their fin-slapping and waited in silent expectation.

back the way we had come and I, shaken, turned to follow.

"That was unbelievable," I cried. "I have never felt such joy, such laughter. The sandwalker seemed to echo all the laughter of the sea and, in doing so, sent it back ten-fold."

"See," laughed the old dolphin, "the sandwalker is not all bad. He cannot do what we do and we, in some small part, share all with him. In turn, we learn from these creatures and in some measure are returned with knowledge of their souls and spirits." "But now," interrupted the fat whale, "you shall meet our greatest discovery, Sharing, for she comes."

I leaped high into the water and spun about but saw nothing. "How do you know she is coming?" I asked. "There are no sandwalkers here."

"Ah," admonished the whale, "you have not learned to listen with your heart. Even now we can feel her coming to us, for her heart sings of the joy of our communication. Look! Even as we speak, she comes."

I spun in the water and there on the smooth dryside was a sandwalker who looked no different than the others I had seen before. This was the great communicator? This was to be the salvation of the dryside? She had golden kelp that waved about her head. Her face, mobile as all sandwalkers', was beaming, twisted as it was in their odd contortions. When she reached the edge of the pool, she waved her puny fins in an odd fashion as if waving or slapping the dryside air.

"Look," said the old dolphin, "she wishes us a joyful morning and prays the Song will be sung."

"You've eaten a too-long dead fish," I said. "She has done nothing more than wave her fins to ward off a bug or to cool her skin."

Then, in a watery explosion, the five dolphin breached from the center of the pond like a giant water flower. Just as they turned in the air for the drop back to the surface, the fat whale exploded up, clearing his own massive size once over and then fell crashing back into the water. The sandwalkers nearly went crazy, their laughter ringing and their souls almost singing as they leaped to their puny fins and slapped and slapped.

I wanted more. I wanted to be a part of this joy, this laughter giving, but that was not to be. My companions, laughing and chortling, dove down

The others laughed, "That is how she speaks, with her fins."

"Then," I continued defiantly, "tell her to set me free. Tell her I am with child and must return to the sea and my mate who waits for me."

"Be patient, Laughter Ring," admonished the whale, "for she can only hear us and sense the Song, if you would, when she is in the water. Wait and watch, for you shall see."

❦

I waited and watched skeptically as Sharing dove crisply into the water. The others swam to her, and I followed, doubt clouding my thoughts. The old dolphin slowly began to speak, "We, your friends, will sing to you the Song of the Sea."

I listened carefully but could hear no answer. Sharing neither said nor sang anything. Instead, she began moving her fins in the water.

"She says she is ready to listen with open heart to all that can be sung this day."

"Carp bile!" I said disgustedly, "You have all been too long captive in this prison. The water is silent as she speaks."

"You listen wrong, pregnant dolphin," retorted the whale impatiently.

"How can I listen wrong?" I continued, undaunted by their display of stupidity, "I listen as I always have—with all my sensing devices. I have heard the hard-shells creak as they open to feed. I have heard a fish's tail as it gently sweeps the water. But I have heard nothing from this sandwalker who pretends to have knowledge of the Song of the Sea."

"You have heard nothing," snapped one of the dolphin, "because you don't know how to listen with your heart. You, in your own way, are as deaf as Sharing. Watch her fins move. Each movement is a note. Put all the notes together and you have song. Maybe not as beautiful as the Song of the Sea but a song just the same."

I watched closely as the sandwalker moved her fins again in the water. Though it was pretty and quite poetic, I still could hear nothing.

The whale continued to translate this unheard conversation, "She asks of you. She asks how you feel. She asks of the baby you carry in your womb. How else would she know of the baby if she could not speak to us?"

"Easy," I snorted in disgust at this deception. "Anyone could see that I am pregnant, either that or I am as grossly obese as you!"

The old whale's eyes opened wide in shock of the insult thrown. Carefully he turned back to Sharing and spoke slowly, "The dolphin does not believe. The dolphin thinks this is all a lie. She seeks proof."

Once again the sandwalker began to wave her arms and to twist the tiny separate fins on fins. As she moved, the whale spoke her movements. "She says you were captured some brief tides ago by several shell-sharks that cornered you in a shallow bay. She says you were lifted upon a great ship and carried closer to the shore. She says you were flown by a great steel bird to this place of ponds. She says you were examined and then placed in an isolation pool. She says you play with your food like a child."

My skin burned with embarrassment at the final comment, and my blood rushed with excitement. There was no way the dolphin or whale could know how I was brought here. There was no way the dolphins or whale could know how I was examined. This sandwalker, this Sharing, could speak and, better still, she could listen.

Shamed now, my speaking tone softened, and I gently asked, "When, then may I leave this place, to join my mate? I am with child, and the birthing will be soon. It is my desire to birth in the open sea. How soon? How soon?"

Sharing looked at me with her tiny bright sandwalker eyes. Once again, like when I was first

The sandwalker seemed to echo all the
laughter of the sea and, in doing so,
sent it back ten-fold.

captured, I could feel the empathy, the compassion, the softness of spirit of this complex creature. She moved her fins poetically and slowly to the whale and other dolphins who readily translated for me.

"She says you shall be set free. If not by all, then by her alone. But she says you cannot leave now. You will not be freed until after the baby is born."

"But why not now?" I wailed in frustration. "Why must the child be born here?"

Again the sandwalker's hands moved slowly in the water. "She says you were examined. The child must be birthed here, for there is something wrong. The child is twisted inside you. If you birth in the open sea, alone, the child will die and so will you."

I lay still in the water, my child's heart beating quietly next to mine. Should I believe? Dare I not believe that this sandwalker has soul, has spirit? Of all that is holy, what was I to do?

The decision was made that I would stay, though my heart yearned to escape and seek Little Brother. It was not an easy decision, for I had never had a baby before and I did not know what to expect. I felt anxious enough this first time without alien life forms warning me of anticipated problems. Finally, I gave in to my fears of the unknown.

During these few but many tides, I partially came to know the sandwalker who was called Sharing.

Counting the tides themselves became a monstrous problem, for these sterile waters where we were kept did not move at all. The waters lay perfectly still, unaffected by the nights of the silverside or of starlight bright. I soon was taught to count and think in other strange rationales, but I continued to count in tides out of stubborn pride rather than the *new* daylight cycle system.

Sharing came daily to the living pool just after the early throwing of the dead fish. She stayed in the pool with me for nearly half of every tide while the other dolphins and the whale translated, and I learned the gentle nuances in the odd way that she spoke. I began to watch carefully the way her fins waved and formed word pictures.

Her face was more expressive than I could have imagined. Occasionally, she stretched her mouth in an odd grimace, showing her teeth. The first time, I thought she was preparing to attack, for it was not unlike the sharp-fin as he prepares to swallow something whole. But her mouth was small, and her teeth were blunt and looked ineffective for doing more than grinding stones.

Through talks with Sharing, the sandwalkers became an even greater enigma than they had been before. Word by word, I learned of them and their odd ways. Sharing explained that she wished to know more of the Song of the Sea and how it was sung and recorded. The whale knew of it but was not a scribe and only knew personal melodies. I, on the other hand, had swum with Harmony and remembered much of the Song.

I was selective in what I told her. Often the whale or my fellow dolphin questioned my failure to give her complete answers. I had seen many evils performed in my travels throughout the seas, for the most part by the sandwalker. Although I came to have a strong friendship with Sharing, in the beginning I continued my editing.

She told my companions she would add my ramblings to her collection. Sandwalkers seemed to be obsessed with collecting things. Things were everything. They had vast collections of woven weeds that they draped over their bodies. Sharing told us the sandwalkers had to possess and the thought of sharing was a horror to them far worse than the end . . . the beginning. All of the sandwalkers appeared to feel this way—that is, except Sharing who for some reason possessed the philosophy of the whale and dolphin.

Sandwalkers didn't migrate or wander free, but rather lived their lives in tiny caves that were constructed by themselves and not by nature. They had even constructed the ponds in which we swam. I learned that the shell-shark was not a natural phenomenon of the dryside but rather was constructed, too. Their ability to construct seemed to be the major difference between the sandwalker and us who sing in the sea.

Their counting was another oddity separating the sandwalker for ALL THAT IS RIGHT IN THE WORLD. They had five little fins on each of two upper fins, so all their counting was based on the unit ten. Time was not measured in tides but rather by the cycle of the golden light. Each day represented approximately two tides.

They developed a system of rewards which were collected and sometimes hoarded. These rewards were stored and used in exchange for other things to collect. They all were rewarded somehow for daily movements, and even Sharing was rewarded for talking to us in the ponds. Odder still was that the other sandwalkers did not truly believe Sharing spoke with us at all. But they still rewarded her for doing it.

All the sandwalkers' learning was not taught in song and passed on from father to son or mother to daughter. Young sandwalkers were taught to memorize vast bodies of information. But the sandwalkers who taught them were not rewarded much at all and collected very little in their lives. These collections were the measure of the value of their lives as they passed at the end . . . the beginning. Oh, sandwalkers were odd indeed.

I was shocked to learn the sandwalker felt love and had many ways to express it. Some even believed in a form of ALL THAT IS RIGHT IN THE WORLD. Maybe there was a greater tie binding us together than had been sung before.

🐚

All this knowledge, as given to me by Sharing, somehow had to be passed on to Harmony and the conclave that was soon to gather. The other dolphin and the whale knew of the importance.

This knowledge should never be given to the Narwhal alone to be used in their devious plan; rather Harmony must know all of the truth.

I soon was able to "listen" to Sharing without translation, and she understood me as well. Daily, she brought us more of the long-dead fish.

Finally one day in disgust, I asked, "Why do you and other sandwalkers throw the long-dead fish in the water? Why cannot we have real food?"

Sharing moved her fins in the water in her odd signing way and said, "But these are real food."

"They are capable of sustaining," I countered in disdain, "but they are hardly real food. Would you, Sharing, eat of them?"

Her mouth twisted in her odd way as she said, "No, but we have a strange way of eating that would not suit you. Better still, I will show you."

She crawled from the pool and soon came back with a large container. From it she took a long reddish cylinder that looked, of all things, like a sea slug, dried and stiff. "Taste of this," she said, and popped the still warm object in my mouth.

I swallowed and then spat all back into the water. "What was that?" I gagged, "It was warm, not cool like sweet meat. It cannot be food."

Once again Sharing's mouth twisted in her odd grimace of delight. "There are some of us who do not think of this as food either, but still many eat of it constantly. It is called a hot creature who is furred and walks on four fins," she signed.

"But," I protested, "this hot creature who is furred and walks on four fins did not taste alive! It did not even taste of meat."

Many burps and gasps escaped Sharing's lips now as she tried to explain that a creature who is furred and walks on four fins was a friend of the sandwalker, a bringer of great joy and laughter.

"Sandwalkers are beasts!" I sang. "Not only do they try to kill all in the sea, they eat their friends."

With fins flashing, Sharing tried to explain to me that the hot tube was not a furred four-fin but rather was made of a large four-fin that schooled like our food fish, the tuna and split-tail. This large four-fin ate the seaweed that grew on the dryside. This was all very confusing and made my head spin, so filled was it with great knowledge.

Over the next several tides I learned more and more from Sharing, and she from me. I was the first she had met who had traveled afar in the seas. I was the first that had shared friendship with a whale, such as Harmony, and experienced first-hand the THOUSAND DEATHS OF THE SANDWALKER.

But in all I explained to Sharing, I told her not of the great conclave. For the conclave's ultimate purpose was to rid the seas and the earth itself of the sandwalker once and for all. I knew not how Sharing would react to her race's demise. I knew not if Sharing, once knowing the truth, would help me escape the ponds and return to the sea. Therefore, in fear that the truth might be likened to one who was friend to a sharp-fin—friend one moment, food another—I maintained silence.

⁂

During one session, a spasm wracked me so hard it spun me in circles, leaving me dazed.

"It has begun," excitedly sang the other dolphin. "The child within wants out."

Sharing splashed over to me and comforted me as best she could. I recovered my breath, only to be wracked a moment later by another convulsion, stronger yet. Of all that is holy, what was I to birth, a whale? The pains continued and then as quickly as they had started, they subsided like the blank hole in the middle of a storm.

"It has passed," I cried in relief, "but the birth will be within this tide."

"I will go," signed Sharing, "and bring other sandwalkers to help me lift you from the water to take you where we can help."

"No!" I exclaimed, "My child will be born in the sea, even this sterile sea. It can be no other way!"

*"Taste of this," she said, and popped
the still warm object in my mouth.*

Sharing signed there was great danger and the baby and I both could die. But I resolutely defied her. My child would be born in the sea or not be born at all. The little sandwalker was agitated but understood my resolve.

Comforting melodies were sung by the other dolphins, and the whale sang bits and pieces of the Song of the Sea. Some time later two other sandwalkers came to help Sharing.

She asked how I felt and I told her that, although the child still moved within me, I had not been wracked by new pains. She signed that the others would have come sooner except there was an oddity in the ponds. She signed curiously, "Yet another dolphin has been brought to these ponds. This is an odd dolphin and . . ."

Before she could continue, once again, my body seemed to explode with pain. The twisting, muscle-tensing pain stiffened me; then, as quickly as it had come, the pain disappeared like a wave passing in the sea. The first wave was followed by another, and yet another.

"The time is soon!" I groaned.

"Oh, dear little dolphin," Sharing waved, "I hope you are doing right to stay in the water. We will help, but it will be very difficult and dangerous." The nervous anticipation and the silence that ensued was broken by an incessant hammering at the other end of the pool. Something or someone kept throwing himself at the gate.

"What was that?" I asked.

"That," signed Sharing, "was the odd dolphin I spoke of. The odd thing is he wanted to be caught even though we didn't want to catch him."

The pain began to well again, but even through the pain my eyes opened wide. It must be.

"Quickly!" I cried. "Let him come near. Hurry!"

Sharing seemed confused at this request but finally signed to another sandwalker, who fiddled with a great smooth-stone ring on the edge of the dryside. The water at the end of the pool surged, and the new dolphin swam through the opening.

Sharing and the other sandwalkers were rudely bumped as this interloper smashed his way to my side. I turned my head to the most lovely sight in all the sea, for there was Little Brother. Then quiet settled over me and all went black.

EXODE

I awoke in a deep and twisted fog. The clouds that normally lightly grazed the waves now were locked inside my mind. My sight was blurred by the rain within. Shell-shark and sandwalker danced together upon the water in their purpled splendor.

Twin Harmonys leaped from the soul of the sea and never came down. The world as a whole spun around me until I finally had to close my eyes tight to stop this vision of fright.

I slowly opened my eyes again and saw nothing, nothing at all. Now the world was devoid of all life. Then I looked again, for the world was not devoid of life, it was only that I could see nothing but darkness. My heart began to hammer in my chest, for surely I was blind, but then the fog cleared.

I found myself bathed in the cool of nighttime with those familiar bits of glitter scattered about the heavens. My head pounded with an ache like I had never felt before, and I breathed deep to exhale whatever poison I had somehow drawn into my system.

My body settled down, and I began to hear the silence and feel the stillness of the sterile ponds. Odd dryside sounds echoed pleasantly in the night. It was then that I remembered the dream—or had it been real?—the blinding, twisting pain of the beginning of birthing and the memory that somehow I had been found by Little Brother. Or was that, too, part of the dream?

I tried to twist around and found that not only could I not move, I could feel nothing of my lower extremities. That's why I was left alone. I was paralyzed, left to die. But what of the child? I could feel nothing move within my womb. Surely the child had died as Sharing had warned.

"The child! The child!" I wailed. "My child is dead and I am dying."

As if in answer to my lament, light lanced like a knife into my eyes, blurring my sight once again with purple splotches and dancing green clouds. Like sunrise, in the blink of an eye, where there was dark before there was now light, but not the warm golden light of the sun.

Out of this mottled dream of colored clouds and bright lights danced a vision of Little Brother. I feared for my sanity, so vivid the hallucination. But what was dream vanished, and what was not remained, and there before me truly was my beloved Little Brother. He swam to me cautiously, concern restraining his movements. I wanted so badly to leap to his side, but I was still paralyzed. That was no dream.

Realizing that I was fully awake and had regained my senses, Little Brother gushed of love and delightful endearments that under normal conditions he wouldn't be caught in a sharp-fin's mouth saying.

I hushed him quiet, then said somberly, "I don't know how you came to be here, but Sharing, the sandwalker, will aid in your escape. The baby has died within, for I can no longer feel it, and I am paralyzed—no better than dead. Go from me, my love. Save yourself and seek the conclave. For I have discovered that the Narwhal have done much evil to the Song of the Sea.

Little Brother looked at me as though I had gone quite daft. "Leave without you? Not hardly."

"But I am frozen in my body and cannot move nor feel. The baby does not move within me—it is dead. Please, for the sake of all that is holy in the sea, save yourself and allow me to join the end . . . the beginning with some sense of dignity."

"I'll give you dignity, indeed," he snorted, "and I'll give you no rest either. You don't feel the child, for it was birthed three tides earlier. It is a she and she is now with Sharing waiting your awakening to be fed the true nurturing that only a mother can give."

"That is wise," I answered gravely. "Even though I am paralyzed, for the brief time I may have left, I can nurture my child."

"What kind of carp bile is this, 'all the time I have left'?" he laughed.

"Well," I sniffed indignantly, "I am paralyzed and will only be good for returning to sea as food for others."

"Paralyzed in the brain only," chortled Little Brother. "You are suspended in some contraption created by the sandwalker so that you wouldn't drown as you slept. As you began the birthing, the child was twisted. Rather than killing you both, the sandwalker stuck you with a silvery spine of some prickly thing and you went fast asleep."

Little Brother paused, then continued, "With the sharpest of stones, she sliced you open neatly and out popped our child. These sandwalkers, though evil incarnate, are a clever lot and they put you back together again as if you had not been torn. As you slept, you have nearly completely healed. In but a group of tides you will be fit to swim the seas, a bit slower than before, but then you were never that fast."

"You just wait," said I, "I'll show you slow."

We laughed together as in the time of our innocence, for we seemed much changed. Finally I stopped and remarked, "It is tradition that the child be named as soon as she touches the waters of life. We are late, but I will devise some name appropriate to the situation."

Little Brother twisted uncomfortably in the water and said a bit awkwardly, "Uh, well it seems that the, uh, child is already named. I, uh, well,

"Giggles," I whispered softly,
"Giggles, a tiny uncontrollable laugh."

when she slid into life, she did so with such joy that Sharing called our child Giggles. That is what she has been called since."

"Giggles," I whispered softly, "Giggles, a tiny uncontrollable laugh."

"We can change it!" blurted Little Brother. "Although it is tradition that the first words spoken at birth are the child's to carry through life, we can surely change it. Other traditions are changing so fast around us, I'm sure no one will notice."

"Change it!" I protested. "Change the most perfect name in all the seas? Never! Think of it—ours is the first dolphin to be named at birth by a sandwalker. Oh, she is bound to greatness."

As if to punctuate my statement, I felt a tiny splash and heard my first giggle from Giggles. It was the sound of tinkling shells on stilled waters. It was a wave broken on a pebbly shore and pulling back to sea. It was delight! As if she knew she was the focal point of our lives, she swam to the center of the pool "blooping" tiny breaches that caused my heart to nearly stop in love, admiration, and pride. She swam, punctuating every stroke with a giggle. It was obvious that Sharing had done well with her birth name.

My baby swam for a time, showing off and exploring every nook and cranny of the smooth-stone pool. Finally she came back to where I lay. She nosed about me. Sensation began to return to my body as her tiny snout poked me here and there. After a moment, Giggles began to suckle, filling herself with all the goodness I had to offer. My body warmed with the pride of motherhood.

I looked at Little Brother, and he looked at me as we spoke in quiet whispers. The baby nursed and then fell asleep. We were a family.

"How did you come to be here?" I finally asked, "and what of the conclave and the message that needs be sent to all who sing in the sea?"

"One thing at a time," he laughed. "First and most important, the message of the conclave is being passed, even as we rest, down the full surface of the sea. Right after I left you, I found a pod of great grey whales and a group of gabby dolphin. Both are moving the message down. All the waters now ring with the great migration, as all who are able and even many who are not, swim up the world to the gathering—the conclave."

"You must know," I said, "I have discovered the Narwhal have withheld knowledge from the Song of the Sea for their own purpose, to strengthen their argument for the THOUSAND DEATHS OF THE SANDWALKER. Through Sharing, I have learned that the sandwalkers are not all bad. Although they do not sing as we sing, it is only because they have never learned to listen."

"I, too, have noted the kindness and the compassion," said Little Brother, "but I will not forget the horrors I have seen in the sea. I will not forget the nets of kelp that kill far, far to the other side of the sea. I will never forget the magnitude of the useless slaughter of the whales and the death of their Song. No, my sweet, we will carry the knowledge we hold and present it to Harmony. The ultimate decision as to the fate of the sandwalker shall be that of the conclave."

❦

We softly floated in gentle silence, satisfied in the simple presence of one another, and then my memory was jogged again. "My dear mate," I teased, "you seem to dodge and avoid the question of how you came to be here in the ponds."

Little Brother laughed in that comfortable way of his and then told this story.

"After passing the message of the conclave on to the dolphin and great greys, I came back to the cove where I had left you, only to find it empty. Empty but not quite, for there were shell-sharks floating with their kelps draped in the water, and one old furred flipper-fin who remembered you had been there. He said you had been eating everything in sight when you were cornered in a shallow part of the cove and lifted into a great shell-shark that quickly swam away.

"I tried to follow, but the seas were quiet and I knew not which way to go. Finally, my mind discovered a great plan. If you had been captured and taken, then I, too, would be captured and taken away. If you were dead, then I would be dead, for life is quite empty without you."

He paused as he spoke looking at me with great tenderness and concern before he continued.

"I went to the first of the shell-sharks that floated in the bay and danced on my tail for them, but they were not interested and tried to shoo me away. I breached. I called, but no one wanted me.

"I became very still, so that I would make an easier prey for capture but no one would take me.

I resolved that if they wouldn't reach for me, I would reach for them. I swam about gaining speed, dove, breached high above a small shell-shark, and easily fell within.

"Unfortunately, my breaching and fall caused the shell-shark to fill with water, and the sandwalkers jumped from their shell. They had not captured me; I had captured them. I tried over and over, but the small shell-sharks filled too easily with water.

"With my plan still shakily intact, I swam out in the deeper water and found a much larger shell-shark. Surely it would be able to support my weight without sinking. I dove deep and surged to the surface in a mighty breach. Once again, my plan was thwarted by my own judgment—I had assumed the shell-shark was lower in the water than it really was. I crashed into the side of that hard-sided beast and nearly knocked myself silly.

"My attempts had not gone unnoticed, and the shell-shark slowed so that the sandwalkers could watch my odd behavior. I shook sense back into my head and dove very, very deep. With every bit of strength I could muster, I shot to the surface like a bubble eager to burst. Higher than I had ever breached before, I left the water, nearly to fly.

"I looked down and there way far below me was the shell-shark. I fell like a rock and smacked on its hard back. The air was forced from my lungs, and all faded to black.

"I awoke some time later to find myself here. It was only at today's early tide that Sharing told me that the sandwalkers on the shell thought me crazed, so I was brought here."

I laughed at Little Brother's story until my sides ached with over-use. It felt so good to laugh again. Giggles woke with a tiny laugh, then fell back to sleep. "But then," I sang eagerly, "you, too, have learned to speak the odd language of Sharing?"

"Yes," he replied arching proudly. "She says I am the fastest student she has ever taught."

My retort was interrupted by Sharing who had come to the edge of the pond. She asked in her odd-finned way how I was feeling. When I told her feeling was returning, she released the restraint that had kept me afloat. Then she slipped into the water and examined my body.

"You are healing well," she signed. "In two tides, we will take you all back to the sea and set you free."

My eyes glistened as I realized that once again we would be free. I thought of telling her of the conclave, the meeting called by Harmony to discuss the fate for all time of the sandwalker. But I didn't know if I should risk telling even one such as Sharing. I remained silent.

As the next tide turned and rolled unseen by us, I was filled with melancholy at my decision not to tell Sharing of the conclave. When we were alone, Little Brother and I discussed the merits of the situation but he was just as confused as I.

I sought out the others, the dolphin and the whale. They felt that I was right. Sharing should not know of the conclave which was called to discuss the future of the sandwalker.

Sharing's allegiance had to be with her own kind. If she knew, the conclave could springboard all the seas into a battlefield of sandwalker versus they who sing. Without the advantage of surprise, the creatures who live in the sea would be wiped from the memory of the waters by the very clever sandwalker and their coveted possessions.

But the decision was not made without regret, and we could sense that Sharing felt something was amiss. Even with the intrigue, we loved her and her stories that had never been heard by our kind before. I'm sure the feeling was reciprocal as we told her the carefully edited truth.

❧

There was a sense of excitement in the pond on our final day—a sense of adventure, of loss, of gain. The dolphin were the first to come and wish us well in our travels.

"Go now to the conclave," they cried. "Carry the truth of the sandwalker. Tell of their great achievements and even greater failures. Tell that the sandwalker does have soul, although they may never learn to sing the Song. Tell of the Narwhal's deception—how they have held melodies back—and of the sandwalker's learning."

With that the dolphin pulled back and the fat whale moved forward.

"I wish," sang he, "that I had a beautiful song to sing but my voice is rusty and I can now barely hum. I, too, wish you a safe journey and a part of me wishes I could travel with you. A conclave of all the singers in the sea has never been called, and it would be a wondrous sight indeed to see everyone brought together, united as they will be. But I must stay here. Perhaps the sandwalker can be taught conscience and understanding of the delicate balance of the dryside and the sea. Go now, my friends, and may ALL THAT IS RIGHT IN THE WORLD watch over you in your travels."

Silence pervaded the pond as we sang not a word, but instead felt the presence of one another. In time, Sharing came to the pond. It was as if she had known our need for farewell and had purposely left us alone. She slipped into the water and explained what would happen and how we would be freed. She said the other sandwalkers did not truly believe she could speak with whale or dolphin. They felt communication with us was futile. We were the clowns, the jokesters, the merrymakers of their strange circus.

The stick puffed a bit of cloud
followed by a loud sound
that reverberated through the water . . .

She said if the other sandwalkers had truly believed we could think and talk, we would never be set free. Dear Sharing, the first sandwalker ever who talked with the singers of the sea.

Sharing climbed from the water and signaled other sandwalkers to push the strange carriers that would move us on the dryside. I urged Giggles to drink deeply of my milk, for while being moved, any such actions would be impossible. As she suckled at my side, I sang to her consoling songs.

But Giggles and I were bound together in the weed weavings, and her closeness to me allayed her fears. I could feel her heart pounding as we were lifted onto the carriers.

We were left there on the edge of the dryside pool as Little Brother was loaded onto his carrier. Together we were moved through great caves and caverns of the dryside. To my shock and delight, we were not taken to the great shell-shark bird but were lifted from the carriers into yet another variation of a shell-shark.

Sharing knelt on her lower fins between Little Brother, Giggles, and me, constantly bathing us with a large soft sponge soaked with the waters of life. After much thumping and clanking, we began to move as if on water but only rougher. We bounced and jostled into the noisy, confusing world of the dryside. Acid burning smells assailed our senses, and we were all numbed by the lack of air. Honkings of great beasts and the roars of other dryside shell-sharks made speech of any kind impossible. But through it all, Sharing soothed us with guttural humming that held great emotion. Once again, I considered singing to her of the conclave, but I still was undecided.

After what seemed like tide after tide but was much shorter than that, the air took on a sweeter smell. Little Brother and I arched our backs in excitement, for the smell could be nothing more than the sea itself.

The shell-shark came to an abrupt stop, and once again we were carefully lifted high over the sides and onto the back of a floating shell that hummed in excitement. These were smaller shells than the ones that had captured me originally and were uniquely formed. Their sides felt almost dolphinlike and were as soft as a fat whale's.

Giggles and I were laid in one, and we watched as Little Brother was dropped in another. Sharing rushed about the tiny shell, fussing with strands of kelp, and then reclined at the back of the boat. The shells roared, and we swam out in the water.

As we plowed through the waves, we saw the other shell racing alongside and Little Brother arching himself so his face was full into the wind. He loved speed; this must have been pure ecstasy.

We traveled for some time, and then the shell became quiet-still. Sharing began to sign as fast as her fins could move. She told me that beyond the dryside was a school of dolphin heading up into the seas. There were pods of whale and flipper-fin that were all strangely moving in one direction. She asked if I knew the meaning of this strange occurrence. I guiltily replied that I didn't know. She stared at me, seeming to know that a secret stood between us like a great wall.

She rolled me into the sea and, after I was in the water, slid Giggles in beside me. I turned to my friend who slipped into the water. She signed slowly, "You will be well. Your wound of childbirth will soon heal with no complications."

Raindrops spilled from her eyes and joined the waters. "Stay in this cove until you are acclimated with the sea once again," she continued. "Giggles will grow stronger every day."

Finally, my heart could stand no more, and I blurted, "Oh, Sharing, we will miss you so, but we must now join the others of our kind."

Sharing climbed back onto the shell and turned and headed back to the dryside. I was quite sad as she floated away. Giggles was frightened at the vastness of the sea and hovered by my side. Little Brother looked at us and realized he had a morale problem in his growing pod. He turned and swam quickly away without a word.

He soon returned, gripping a tuna-tail. "Here, you may eat this now, or wait until it is very dead like the food fed to us by the sandwalkers. I understand how very fond of those fish you were."

He tossed me the morsel, then with a flip of his tail, he surged away again. How sweet the meat of the sea! I felt content, as Giggles satisfied herself with her mother's milk. Soon Little Brother returned with still another juicy fish.

I asked, "How did you catch such fish so quickly?"

"Easy," he chuckled. "A sandwalker floats in a shell-shark dragging his twisted kelp. In the twists are all sorts of fish." With that, he tossed me the fish and swam back to the shell-shark.

My belly full, I watched lazily as Little Brother swam close to the shell-shark and dove to steal another fish. As he rose with his prize clutched in his jaws, the sandwalker suddenly leaped upright in the shell and pointed a smooth stick at my mate. The stick puffed a bit of cloud followed by a loud sound that reverberated through the water, and then the water went ghostly still and flat.

With no thought of Giggles, I rushed to Little Brother who lay still in the water. Fortunately, Giggles stayed where she was. Little Brother's eyes glazed, and he didn't appear to be breathing. Blood poured from a wound in his side, and the sea ran red. I swam toward the sandwalker who still stood on his shell holding the stick of death. He slowly raised the stick and pointed it directly at me.

"Harmony and the Narwhal are both right," I snarled. "All sandwalkers need to be eliminated from the earth."

With slimy rock eyes, the sandwalker began to clench one of his tiny fins holding the stick, and I prepared to die. I don't know if I blinked, but in that moment of time, a new sound broke the tension—the roaring hum of another shell-shark.

The sandwalker turned and saw the shell bearing down on him. Assuming it to be a friend, he turned and again raised the stick. But the other shell rammed the shell-shark, hitting the stick-wielding sandwalker full force.

The evil creature that killed Little Brother was thrown over the side and into the water. The attacking sandwalker turned its tiny shell towards me and the body I coveted. From the shell, a sandwalker leaped into the water and was upon us before I could take any defensive action, but no action was necessary for it was our beloved Sharing. She grabbed Little Brother and pulled him to her shell where she looked at the wound on his side. Satisfied that the body was being cared for I sought Giggles and gathered her to me. Together we sadly swam back to Sharing who still hovered over him.

"I cannot believe it!" I cried. "Little Brother died seeking to cheer me up with the fresh fish. Oh, that silly fool. I loved him so."

"He's not dead," said Sharing, piercing his skin with a prickly-point.

His eyes opened and he asked, "Am I dead?" Sharing stabbed him again with the prickly-point. Little Brother answered with the slap of his tail on the water, as he cried out, "Ow, that stings!"

Sharing cradled him firmly in her scrawny fins and dabbed at the wound. Little Brother continued complaining, but his whining was pure music to my ears. Only *live* dolphin can complain the way he was. The bleeding stopped, and Little Brother began to move tentatively about, gaining his bearings. Sharing signed, "He was only grazed by the stone that flies with power."

"My dear friend," I sang in humility, "you would attack one of your own to save a life in the sea?"

"Yes," she signed, "the sandwalker must learn he does not hold dominion over living things. He must learn life is to be cherished within the laws of Nature and ALL THAT IS RIGHT IN THE WORLD."

I paused, staring at this sandwalker who had saved me not only once but twice, and also saved my child and my mate. She must know of the great conclave.

"For you are more than a sandwalker.
In a small way, you have learned to sing
the Song of the Sea."

"There is much we have not told you," I sighed. "The dolphin and whale who wait for you in the sterile ponds came to you, not by capture, but out of their own choice. As you learn from them, so they learn from you. All this knowledge has been passed to a whale or dolphin that was to be set free. Once freed, they carried this bit of Song to the mysterious Narwhal in the colder waters."

"I knew it!" signed Sharing excitedly. "I just knew there was more to all of this."

I continued, "Something wondrous is about to occur—a conclave of all the singing creatures in the sea. There has never been such a gathering except at the beginning when ALL THAT IS RIGHT IN THE WORLD allowed us to be as one."

"You must tell me where the conclave is to take place," she enthusiastically waved, "for I must see this with my own eyes and feel the Song as it is truly sung by all who can sing. Please tell me. I will sneak into their presence and no one will know I was there. I will hide. Your secret will be safe with me. Please tell me."

I ignored her and continued, "You must know the reason for the gathering. The great white whale, Harmony, has called for the conclave of all, and all are moving up the seas to the colder place where the Narwhal live. There shall be enacted a plan to save the seas from the greater evil."

Sharing paused and stared at me with those strange, ice-blue eyes. "But what is the greater evil?" she signed.

"The greater evil," I continued, "is you, the sandwalker."

"What is the plan?" she asked.

"I know not," I sighed. "Only Harmony knows. I know his plan will call for the end of the lives of all the sandwalkers that walk on the dryside."

"Why are you now telling me of this?" asked Sharing.

I paused, looking at Little Brother and Giggles who frolicked in the waters of life. "For you are more than a sandwalker. In a small way, you have learned to sing the Song of the Sea. You must come to the conclave, but not as an interloper or an unwanted guest. You must come as a singer, for a singer you are."

She blinked away tears welling in her eyes as she understood the import of the invitation. "I will be there," she waved, "I will attempt to bring great learned sandwalkers with me so that they too will understand the Song of the Sea."

Without another word, I swam from her. Little Brother and Giggles joined me, and we quietly swam out to sea to join the others silently moving up the world to the conclave. Would she be there, I wondered? Could she find the place where only singers could dwell? Could Sharing learn the Song and in turn sing it to others? Questions, many, many questions and no answers save for time.

But the Song will be sung in the sea, with or without the sandwalker.